# Making Friends
## with Billy Wong

Also by Augusta Scattergood

*Glory Be*
*The Way to Stay in Destiny*

# Making Friends with Billy Wong

## AUGUSTA SCATTERGOOD

Scholastic Press / *New York*

All rights reserved. Published by Scholastic Press, an imprint of Scholastic
Inc., *Publishers since 1920*. SCHOLASTIC, SCHOLASTIC PRESS, and associated
logos are trademarks and/or registered trademarks of Scholastic Inc.

The publisher does not have any control over and does not assume any
responsibility for author or third-party websites or their content.

Library of Congress Cataloging-in-Publication Data available

ISBN 978-0-545-92425-2

10 9 8 7 6 5 4 3 2 1     16 17 18 19 20

Printed in the U.S.A.   23
First edition, September 2016

Book design by Abby Dening

*This one's for Evie, Lucy, Grant, Chase, and Jay.*
*With love.*

# Chapter 1

All it took to send my summer on the road to ruin was a fancy note and a three-cent stamp. The minute that envelope showed up, Mama was packing my suitcase.

Except for when I asked her for a pimento cheese sandwich at the Esso gas station, I didn't talk the entire way from Texas to Arkansas. When you aren't speaking to the person next to you, five hours and thirty-two minutes is a long, hot car ride. But my mama talked. A lot.

"Your grandmother wants to get to know you, Azalea. She needs your help." She turned off the highway at the sign *Paris Junction Arkansas 3 miles*, and she kept talking. "That's why she wrote that sweet note. You'll be fine."

1

I slumped down and clomped my cowboy boots against the front seat. After a while, I whispered, "You know I'm not good with new people. Why can't you help her?"

"You realize I'd stay if I could."

"I realize no such thing." I crossed my arms and blinked hard to keep from crying.

"My new job's just started and your daddy's on the road." Mama fiddled with one gold loop earring, then with the radio dial, and didn't say her real reasons.

1. I'm not allowed to sit at home by myself while she works. Till I'm twelve. Which I will be next year.
2. She's hardly come back to Arkansas since her own daddy died.
3. Every time she and my grandmother talk on the telephone, my daddy says fireworks start flying!

"What if I miss the Tyler Elementary Back-to-School Picnic?"

"It wouldn't be the end of the world," Mama said.

"Well, it might be the end of *my* world."

Okay, I truly don't care about meeting a bunch of sixth-grade strangers, even if my one true friend, Barbara Jean, swears the picnic will be fun. But I'm not admitting that.

"I'd better not miss riding up front in Daddy's big rig to the Grand Canyon. He promised I could go if I made straight As in fifth grade."

She ignored that and said, "You might find a friend in Paris Junction."

"I have a friend. She's back in Texas." I glanced out the window when we pulled up to #14 Ruby Street, a little blue house with a mailbox out front. "Don't even know what to call my own grandmother! All I have is that one birthday card she sent last April."

"Try Grandma Clark. That's what I called mine." Mama smoothed down her hair and checked her lipstick in the mirror before she stepped into the hot sunshine. She was finished with talking. Finished with me.

I gave up and stomped up the sidewalk to my grandmother's front porch. *After* I slammed the car door hard enough for Daddy to hear clear to Texas.

# Chapter 2

Dragging my suitcase up the sidewalk inch by inch, I smiled a little at the gray-haired lady in a wheelchair. She didn't smile back. No, sir. Not one bit.

But Mama was smiling big enough for all of us. "Look at you, sitting up so nice," my own mama called out in a high, silly voice I didn't recognize. She straightened my grandmother's blue sweater, even though the sun was beating down hot as all get-out. "Sorry you hurt yourself in the garden. Here's Azalea, though. She's excited to help."

Excited, my foot. But Mama nudged me and I edged closer to my grandmother. She held her arm up to a green fern. "Haven't seen you since you were this tall, Azalea."

The way she pronounced my name made me worry she was about to make fun of Daddy naming me after a blooming bush. Which he did when he saw the pink blossoms from the hospital-room window the day I was born.

"Hello, Grandma Clark," I answered, making sure I didn't kick over a flowerpot with my new cowboy boots. Mama grabbed my fingers and my grandmother's and smushed us all together. When the butterfly ring I'd given her dug into my hand, I pulled away, leaving Mama holding on to just my grandmother.

After listening to how dry this summer turned out, we finally stepped into a front hall that smelled like mothballs and furniture polish, and I squeezed my arms in tight. Praying I didn't bump into the whatnot cabinet full of china cats.

My grandmother blotted her rouged cheeks with a lace handkerchief and looked right at me. "Appreciate you being here, but don't expect coddling. Never coddled your mother. Don't plan to start with you. Which I'm sure Johnny Morgan, that daddy of yours, does."

Mama glanced out the front window. Like she was worried our old car might crank itself up, drive away, and leave her here with Grandma Clark bossing *her* instead of me.

"Sorry you hurt your foot," I mumbled.

She took a breath that lifted her shoulders slowly up and down. Straightening the flowered apron covering her lap, she said, "My garden's getting away from me, especially my roses. That's all. Can't do much cooking, either. Don't like to depend on neighbors. Your mother says you cook."

If I didn't, we'd eat a lot of cereal and peanut butter. But I wasn't admitting that to a grandmother I hardly knew. Instead, I answered, "Yes, ma'am, I do."

"Right now, the kitchen's full of casseroles. Not up to my standards, but the neighbors mean well. Let's find something to eat."

Mama answered real quick. "Wish I could, but I can't take tomorrow off from my new job."

I stuffed my hands in my pockets and frowned. "You're not staying for supper?"

She reached out to smooth back a strand of straight hair hanging over my cheek. I pulled away. "Promised your daddy I wouldn't be on the road all night."

Grandma Clark picked up her walking stick and pointed it at my suitcase like it might be escorting a family of dust bunnies into her house. "Then show Azalea your old room, JoBelle. Take the child's valise with you."

Following Mama up the stairs, I slowed down by a wall of photographs. Was I kin to these frowning old people? All I knew about my family was that Mama and Daddy had taken off from Paris Junction the minute their high school principal passed around the diplomas. I touched a crooked frame and stared some more. But Mama was already to the top of the narrow steps. I followed her and shoved my suitcase—my *valise!*—into the little bedroom.

I opened the closet door, then the drawers in the chest by the bed, one by one. "If you leave me here, I might discover some deep, dark secret. Something you don't want me to know."

"Doubt that!" Mama laughed and straightened a picture of a dopey girl herding sheep in a fancy pink dress. "Let's get some fresh air in here."

She opened the window next to the bed, then fussed around with my pedal pushers and blouses, fluffing them up and hanging them in the empty closet. But unless I'm back for the sixth-grade picnic, I'm never wearing my new pedal pushers.

I grabbed the blue dress she'd forced me to bring. "I can unpack myself."

"Sure you can! And I need to start for home. Your grandmother doesn't need me."

7

"You're leaving me in a place full of people I don't know, in a house with a grandma who's practically a stranger? *I* need you," I said.

I did not need to be dropped off in a town where everybody gossips about your business. Least that's why Mama said she left Paris Junction.

She reached out to hug me. "I'll call tomorrow after five when the rates go down. Daddy and me—we'll be back to get you as soon as your grandmother's better. Pinkie swear." She wiggled her finger at me, but I ignored her pinkie and turned around before Mama could so much as *try* to hug me again. Then she was gone.

Pulling back the window shade—just a crack—in what was suddenly my room, I almost chewed a hole in my bottom lip biting back tears. It was hard to look at our old station wagon driving off, leaving me here.

Mama couldn't wait to get back to Texas.

Me neither.


Instead of chasing Mama down the steps, I looked closer at what was now my room. On a shelf, three china cups and saucers and the most beautiful painted plate I'd ever seen were lined up in a neat row. I spit on the edge of my blouse and cleaned the dust off the big plate, dreaming up every excuse to hide out in this room. I opened my sketchbook with *Azalea Ann Morgan's Handwriting Practice* and *Keep Out! Private! This Means You!* written across the top. Even though I did win the school prize for Palmer penmanship, that *Handwriting Practice* was a trick so nobody'd discover my pictures.

On a clean page, I wrote LEAVING ARKANSAS in perfect block letters and doodled a bluebird flying over the Grand Canyon. I tried to copy the purple from the fairies' wings floating around the side of the plate, but there aren't enough colored pencils in the world to match that color. I signed the drawing with a flourishy line to mark the date I came to Paris Junction.

*Azalea Ann Morgan, August 3, 1952.*

Before I finished that flourish, banging started on the banister. Wiping any sign of tears off my face and dust off my fingers, I jumped up so quick, something fell. The plate! Shattered! Could I fix it? Should I show my grandmother? Maybe if she finds out I break things and, really and truly, I don't know a thing about prizewinning roses, she'll send me home.

# Chapter 3

My grandmother stopped knocking her cane against the stair post long enough to ask, "What took you so long?"

I couldn't confess I'd smashed her beautiful plate into a million pieces. "Unpacking," I said quietly.

She looked at me like I'd landed from outer space instead of riding all the way from Texas to help out. She shook her head at my boots. Frowned at my knees banged up from falling out of a tree last week. "Let's get going before it gets too dark to see the tomatoes," she said, turning in her wheelchair.

I followed her to the kitchen.

"Hand me the bread off the counter," she ordered.

"Bread?"

"Stale. For the birds. Keeps them off my blackberries."

I grabbed the bread, and before I could say *get me outta here quick*, my grandmother had wheeled herself toward the back steps. Somebody'd hammered thick wooden handrails so she could get outside without falling—as long as somebody like *me* was holding her up. She clutched that rail and I clutched her shoulder and we struggled down the five steps.

Way out back as far as I could see, everything shot up tall. "Wow, your garden's really something, Grandma Clark," I said, trying her name out loud.

What I thought was, *Who's gonna be taking care of all this?*

She sank into a lawn chair and said, "No rain this past week. You'll get the sprinklers out tomorrow."

Guess that answered my question.

"See that? Pigweed'll take over if you let it. Doc Wiggins told me if I so much as pull up a wayward blade of grass before this heals"—she shook the cane at the white tape winding from her ankle to her toes—"he'll skin me alive and hang me for crow bait in my own backyard."

"Biggest garden I ever saw."

Grandma Clark pointed at a row of what looked like roses. "Most important thing to remember? My prize-winners are here, closest to the house. You do know the difference between a weed and a flower, don't you?"

Even though the truth was *not exactly*, I answered, "Yes, ma'am. Last week, Daddy and me painted two old tractor tires white and planted mums behind our duplex. You should try it. Real pretty."

Grandma Clark sighed, shook her head, and nodded toward the back steps. "Gloves in my gardening box. Watch out for spiderwebs. Bring the bucket for the beans and tomatoes near the side fence."

Scrambling under the wooden steps, I held my breath and hoped to high heaven there wasn't a yellow-jacket nest up under there. I grabbed the gloves and bucket before a gigantic spider bit off my finger. I crawled out quick and went searching for beans by the fence. Instead of beans, I spied something else. A little white house.

Was it a garden shed? A playhouse? Back home, my friend Barbara Jean had a shed full of broken pots and dried-up fertilizer behind *her* house. Grandma Clark's had two windows covered over with thick vines that were starting to creep up the blue door, like nobody had opened it in a while. I put down the bucket and started up the twisty path to my grandmother's chair. "What's in that shed?" I asked. "Maybe a bike or some skates left over from my mama?"

"Stay away from that old place. Not your concern. Nothing inside but crickets and spiders."

Truly, I am not crazy about spiders *or* crickets.

I pulled up weeds and picked beans until daylight almost disappeared and she finally said, "Enough for now, Azalea. Help me up into the house."

Standing on the top step, you could see the all the way to the back fence, the alleyway, a tall tree fanning out over the garden.

An oak tree. Where somebody was sitting. And waving.

I squinted into the last of the evening light. "Is a boy in that tree?"

"Why, that's Billy Wong. His family owns Lucky Foods grocery, where some of my vegetables are sold. Since the Chinese Mission School out on the highway closed, nobody tends their school garden. The Wongs get some of mine." Grandma Clark let go of the railing to wave and call out, "Hello, Billy!"

Chinese school? There was a boy from China in a tree in my grandmother's backyard?

13

"Why's he in that tree?"

"Can't keep the neighborhood children out of it." Grandma Clark drew herself up tall, smiled, and waved again. "He's recently moved to Paris Junction, but I've known the family forever. I suspect Billy'd make a good friend, Azalea."

If my grandmother really knew me or even wanted to know me like her note said, she'd understand I don't need another friend.

"My best friend is Barbara Jean. She's in Texas," I answered quietly.

And truthfully? How could I talk to a boy who looked like he'd just moved here from China?

Glancing back one last time, I saw him and his bright white T-shirt shinnying down the tree. Before I could say *ripe red tomato* three times fast, Billy Wong waved, then disappeared down the alley.

# Inside Lucky Foods Grocery

Since I was old enough to stand on
a wooden fruit crate and roll nickels.
First, at my parents' grocery. Now, at Lucky Foods.
After school.
Most every day.
Weekends, too.
I've worked hard.

Now I run hard, like it's a race, a sprint.
All the way back to Lucky Foods.
I push open the door.
Stop.
Catch my breath.
Great Aunt waits by the cash register.
"Sorry I'm late, Auntie."
"Put on your apron. Evening shoppers coming."
She disappears into her kitchen behind the store.
Smells of pork and onions drift in.
Mix with peppermints on the counter.

Maybe I shouldn't climb trees
to daydream in the clouds.
But high on a tree branch, stories pop wide open.

I tie the white apron around my waist
and straighten pickle jars.
Stories jumping.
Popping.
Waiting to explode
onto the pages of the *Tiger Times*.

*Billy Wong, Hoping-to-Be Cub Reporter for the*
*Paris Junction* Tiger Times *School Newspaper*

# Chapter 4

Back inside her kitchen, Grandma Clark talked about how she'd never put onions in *her* green bean casserole. I didn't care much about onions or the neighbors' casseroles. But I couldn't stop wondering about that Chinese boy in her tree.

"Does your garden take a lot of work?" I finally got brave enough to ask.

She pushed her wheelchair closer to the table and fiddled with the saltshaker. "Don't think you have to do everything. We'll have other garden helpers. Like Billy Wong out there."

"Billy Wong? Other garden helpers?" I whispered, thinking *How soon can I get back to Tyler, Texas?*

Somewhere on our long, boring drive to Arkansas, Mama told me I'd cook and clean. I might run errands. Pull weeds and pick tomatoes. Since I wasn't talking, I didn't ask questions. But honest to goodness, she never said there'd be other helpers.

"At the end of the summer a few neighborhood children help put my garden to bed. Done it since your granddaddy passed on. I try to teach them what not to dig and how to properly clip." My grandmother shook her head at her bandaged-up foot. "After I fell, the call went out that I needed them now."

"Who's coming?" I asked quietly.

"Billy will be here for sure."

"Does he speak English?"

Grandma Clark's head jerked up. "Of course he does." She stared right at my face, frowning. "There'll be others, too. Melinda, a sweet girl who means well. Don't know who all will show up. People come when you need them in Paris Junction."

"Mama told me that." Mama also said she and Daddy couldn't wait to leave a place where everybody watches every move you make. "Back home, I don't even know that many people."

Grandma Clark made a sound that reminded me of my first-grade teacher when we didn't line up straight for recess. "Why on earth don't you know your neighbors at the very least?"

"We've moved a few times."

Grandma Clark clucked again. "Your father always imagines a better job, a bigger house, something waiting around the corner. No way to raise a child."

Good gravy. Was I going to have to talk to strangers, pull up weeds, *and* take up for Daddy all the livelong day? I turned away from my grandmother and checked on the casserole bubbling in the oven. When she pronounced it ready, I served it up. On the kitchen wall, her cat clock tick-tick-ticked away while we quietly ate.

Finally, my grandmother took her last bite of casserole and said, "That wasn't the worst supper I've ever had. At least we have food in the icebox. For now. People in Paris Junction try their best when a neighbor's in need. Your granddaddy always said friends are a true treasure."

"I like to know somebody awhile before making her my friend."

Grandma Clark patted her lips with her napkin, then folded it next to her plate. I'm sure *she* can't imagine spending a single day in a place where a zillion strangers don't come running at the first sign of a sprained toe. "No need to worry. You'll make friends. Be your own, true self."

"Tell the truth and shame the devil, Daddy always says. Being truthful doesn't make me like meeting people, though. Besides, I thought you needed me for garden stuff. Why do we need other helpers?"

"*Stuff* is not a becoming word, Azalea. Don't need help with *stuff*." She pronounced it like a cuss word that needed washing out of my mouth.

After I dried our plates with a white ironed dish towel and my grandmother told me where to stack them, she wheeled into her bedroom. I stood a few feet away, waiting for orders. The real truth? My grandmother kind of scared me.

Grandma Clark slipped into her nightgown, muttering, "We'll get an early start tomorrow. Lots to do." She took off her glasses for the night and squinted. "Come here, Azalea," she said, and my lip trembled more than a little.

I tried to lean away. But she took my hand and pulled me so close I smelled the rose lotion on her wrinkles. "Yes, ma'am?"

"Let's see if you resemble that father of yours." She pulled me closer. "As I feared. Johnny Morgan's devilish blue eyes. Sure as the grass grows, you didn't get your eyes or your height from our side of the family."

"Good night, Grandma Clark," I whispered. I turned off her light and tiptoed to my new room, heart beating fast. I stumbled only once on the creaky stairs.

# Chapter 5

When the sun peeked under my window shade the next morning, I started down the steps. But Mama's voice sneaked into my head, so I listened and pulled a comb through my hair and passed a toothbrush across my teeth.

In Grandma Clark's kitchen cupboards, spices were lined up in order, but I didn't recognize a single box of cereal. I grabbed a banana and a *Ladies' Home Journal* magazine snitched from the coffee table. As I tiptoed outside, I passed my grandmother's room. She was snoring loud.

If I was back in Texas with my friend Barbara Jean like I oughta be, we'd be watching *The Lone Ranger* on her brand-new TV. Then we'd drink lemonade on her porch swing, talking about sixth grade, hoping we'd get Miss Cain for our teacher.

Here in Paris Junction, I stared down the sidewalk, hoping a squirrel would run across the grass. Even a squirrel's better to look at than fancy pictures of tabletop settings. I wanted to fling my grandmother's magazine across the porch! Compared to reading about cake decorating, running through my sprinkler back in Texas with Barbara Jean counts as diving into the deep end of a swimming pool.

But when a car stopped and a short, skinny stranger stepped out, I almost hightailed it inside. I wasn't fast enough. She was on the porch, shifting her pocketbook under an arm and talking.

"This is Mrs. Clark's house," she said, like she was telling me something I didn't know. "And you are?"

Since sooner or later everybody in Paris Junction knows everybody else, I answered, "I'm her granddaughter. Visiting from Texas."

She looked at the front door. "I'm Jane Partridge. Is she available?"

"I'll see." I disappeared inside.

Grandma Clark was twisting the back of her hair into a tight bun and poking it with bobby pins. "I've been awake for hours. Where've you been?"

To be nice, I didn't point out her snoring.

Motioning for the wheelchair, she looked out the window onto the porch. "No doubt Jane Partridge needs something. Hand me my glasses and my hankie."

Good gravy. For an old lady, she had things to learn about please and thank you. I wheeled her into the living room anyhow.

"Wait on the porch, Azalea." My grandmother flapped her hand toward the door, and I got the message. Not that I wanted to *talk* to this person. But in case they said something good, I crouched under the open window, listening. While Miss Partridge and my grandmother blabbed about a boy named Willis Something-or-other, I quietly unraveled a string on a chair cushion.

"You would be doing the county a favor. We hate for this to be blown out of proportion, but there are laws," Miss Partridge was saying. "I suggested he work it off at the grocery store. Mr. Wong wanted no part of that. I gather the boy has a bit of a reputation."

Holy crow. Somebody was in hot water.

Finally, my grandmother answered. "Don't like to be in the middle of Mr. Wong's business."

"If you let him work off his punishment in your garden, Mr. Wong will be satisfied. As will the county judge." Miss

Partridge snapped her purse shut, put the cap on her fat fountain pen, and handed my grandmother a manila folder.

"I could use the help of a strong boy. But with my granddaughter here and the other children coming, I have enough on my hands." Grandma Clark pushed the folder back in the lady's direction.

Miss Partridge must not be one to take no for an answer. "Things aren't going well for the family. You should reconsider."

I saw that folder go back in my grandmother's hand and for a long, quiet minute, all I could hear was the ceiling fan humming on the porch. Then Miss Partridge left as quick as she came. I hopped up and hurried inside, tossing Grandma Clark's magazine on the table, wondering if she would spill the beans about this boy Willis.

"Can I fix you some breakfast?" I asked. But after I nicely made toast and coffee, my grandmother wheeled herself into her bedroom and clicked on the radio.

"Till Mama took her new job, we listened to *The Guiding Light* together all summer long," I said, quiet and hopeful.

"I prefer hearing my stories alone," she answered.

Maybe she'd turn the volume up.

Standing outside her bedroom door, waiting for her

25

radio to warm up, I figured out two things about staying in
Paris Junction.

1. Like it or not, I was going to meet more
   people than I was ever friends with back in
   Texas.
2. Because somebody named Willis was in big
   trouble, my grandmother needed to lie down
   and listen to the radio. Alone.

# Chapter 6

If I pressed my ear against my grandmother's bedroom door, I could almost hear the radio. As soon as *The Guiding Light* announced The End, Grandma Clark summoned me. I handed her a tall glass of sweet tea. She raised an eyebrow. "I take lemon. Remember that. You need to pick up lemons at Mr. Wong's grocery."

"Mr. Wong's grocery?"

"Pay attention, Azalea. You saw his great-nephew Billy in the garden last night."

"The boy in the tree? Are they really Chinese? I never met anybody from China." Wasn't sure I needed to start today, either.

"The family came from there a long while ago. But Billy's from across the river. Shallowater, Mississippi. He's living with his great-aunt and uncle so he can begin school."

"Don't they have schools in Shallowater?" Maybe a town with a name like that wouldn't have much of anything.

"Not schools Billy prefers to attend. He was to go to the Negro school, much inferior. He wasn't allowed to go to the better school, simply because he's Chinese."

I didn't know why so many Chinese people lived here and I sure didn't understand why one school needed to be better than another school or why you couldn't go to whichever school you wanted to. If I paid attention and listened, maybe I'd find out.

"Why are there Chinese people in Paris Junction? Back home, I don't know any foreigners."

"Azalea! Billy's not a foreigner." Grandma Clark's mouth pinched up and she shook her head. "Too many questions. Now, walk to the end of Ruby Street, turn right. Since the fancy grocery by the gas station closed, Lucky Foods is the only food store in town. Otherwise, it's a drive out to the highway." She glanced toward the fat bandage covering her foot. "Even when I can drive, I prefer Lucky Foods. Everybody loves Mr. Wong. He'll help you."

"Is it okay if I look around?"

A quick laugh escaped from my grandmother. "Downtown Paris Junction? That shouldn't take long." She handed me a sack of tomatoes. "Give these to Mr. Wong. Hurry. It'll be busy in there by noon. But I called in my order. He'll put it on my tab."

"So I don't have to talk to anybody?" I didn't want to be rude. But how'd she expect me to understand an old man from China when I didn't speak a word of Chinese?

"Of course you'll talk. And if you see Billy, tell him we're looking forward to having him help. Tomorrow, before it gets hot as the dickens. And one more thing." Grandma Clark grasped my bare arm. "Mind your manners. Be friendly to Billy."

"Yes, ma'am."

But truly, what would I say? Would this Billy Wong boy want to talk to me? Did we speak the same language? I wasn't so great at talking to *ordinary* boys back home— boys who didn't look like they'd just arrived from some faraway country. Mama says I'll get over that talking-to-boys thing. I doubt I'll get over it this summer in Paris Junction, Arkansas.

———

Not counting stopping to wave back to a man sweeping the sidewalk and the time I wasted turning left instead of right in front of Ward's Drugstore, walking to town took ten minutes. Even with a stop in front of a store advertising Whitman's Samplers, the candy Daddy brings home. Oh boy, could I go for a chocolate-covered cherry right now. But a bigger sign on the boarded-up door said *Closed*. Shoot.

Another sign in a window said the Kitty Korner and Dog Delight store sells homemade cupcakes. The library opens at ten, three days a week. Next door, the Paris Junction History Room was shut tight.

Lordy, you could roll a bowling ball down Main Street today and nobody would notice. Not that I'd ever held a bowling ball. I'd probably drop it on my toe and end up like Grandma Clark.

Outside the Lucky Foods grocery store, I took a deep, brave breath. My grandmother said everybody loves Mr. Wong. I didn't know if *I'd* love him. I hoped I could understand him. Maybe he'd hand me our groceries and I could leave. Letting my breath out in a whispery whoosh, I opened the screen door and a bell ting-a-linged.

Holy moly. I'd never seen a store like this! Cereal boxes, cookie boxes, and wooden crates filled with apples and pears were stacked near the front. On the counter, a newspaper lay open to a page with squiggles that made me blink. The Chinese boy from yesterday was nowhere in sight. But voices I couldn't understand swirled around the store. I wanted to run all the way home to Grandma Clark's.

I didn't have time to run. An old Chinese man walked right up. Oh, no! I was going to have to talk! My hands were sweating and not just because it was hot as everything. I tried not to stare at his white apron dotted with blotches that matched the inside of his butcher's case.

Then he smiled! "What can I do for you?" I understood!

I handed him the tomatoes and tried to make my voice strong. "I'm Azalea. Mrs. Clark's granddaughter. These are from her garden."

"Thank you. It is nice to meet you, Azalea." He reached in his apron pocket and held up a piece of paper. "Groceries almost ready."

We walked through the store, picking up milk and cream, a giant square of butter. Mr. Wong had his note from Grandma Clark, and quicker than I could mumble *lemons for tea* three times fast, I was holding my groceries.

That wasn't so terrible.

But then a boy wearing dirty tennis shoes and a shirt that barely covered his belly button pushed his way in. When his eyes cut over to where I was standing, I slipped behind the cereal display. He grabbed a little jar of peanut butter, a bottle of Double-Cola, and a sleeve of Saltines.

Mr. Wong shook his finger. "Be quick!" he said. While Mr. Wong packed his groceries in a sack, sly as anything, the boy stuffed something in his front pocket.

Was it an entire pack of bubble gum? Had he forgotten to pay? Or did that boy outright steal from the Lucky Foods store in plain daylight?

Mr. Wong opened the door to the sidewalk, motioned for him to leave right now.

Tucking Grandma Clark's groceries in the crook of my arm, I walked into the bright sunshine. Down Main Street past the gas station, the boy balanced his sack on his bike's handlebars. After he gulped down a big swig of Double-Cola, he pushed his kickstand up and pedaled past the boarded-up store that used to sell Whitman's Samplers.

What had made Mr. Wong mad enough to tell him to leave? Where was he going in such a hurry? But even if I did wonder about the boy and even if I *could* run real fast, the bike zoomed off. Really and truly, I did not want to talk to one more person today.

Besides, the milk was getting warm. The butter was close to melting. And I had a grandmother waiting for lemons and dying to boss me around.

# Who Shops at Lucky Foods

From the back of the store
through our half-closed kitchen door
I watch.

A boy barges in.
Wearing a faded yellow shirt.
Skin with a million freckles.
A crew cut so short his ears stick out like a clown.
But he's not cutting up.
He's strutting.

Great Uncle's smile disappears.
"What do you need? Get it and be quick."
The boy picks up crackers, a cold drink.
A jar of peanut butter.

Great Uncle barks, "One dollar twenty-four."
Pennies, dimes, nickels roll from the boy's hand.
He rescues every coin.

Reaches in his pocket for one last quarter.
Slides money across the counter.
Sneers at Great Uncle.
Touches Bazooka bubble gum.
Walks out.

The girl hiding behind the Wheaties leaves, too.

I ask, "Who was that?"

"Mrs. Clark's granddaughter. Very nice.
Boy, name is Willis. Bad influence.
Stay away from him."

Great Uncle's frown says
he wants to string Willis up
like the sausages behind the meat counter.
But he turns back to chopping neck bones
with a meat cleaver.
No more talking.

I grab my apron. The broom.
Sweep up the sawdust flakes
left from this morning's cleaning.

Whisk them across the wooden floor
to the sidewalk.
Send sawdust and a wish flying behind the boy.
A wish that Willis will stay away from Lucky Foods.
Forever.

*Billy Wong, Great Nephew*

# Chapter 7

When I hurried inside with the groceries, the butter hadn't melted.

Grandma Clark pushed her wheelchair close. "What'd you think of our little town?"

Instead of blabbing that Mr. Wong wasn't so friendly to everybody, I opened the icebox and answered, "Tyler, Texas, has more than one street downtown."

"If you're baking cookies and run out of cinnamon, in Paris Junction you can walk to buy it and be back before the cookies are ready," she said.

*If* a million people didn't try to talk to you before you hardly got out the door, I didn't say.

After I fixed our noon meal, put the dishes away, and hung two loads of laundry on the clothesline, I collapsed into a kitchen chair. But when the phone rang, I jumped up.

"It might be Mama! She said she'd call today."

"Don't pick up the phone! Wait for the rings. Long-long short." She counted with a hand tap on the kitchen table. "Remember. I share a party line."

Grandma Clark could have been speaking pig latin. I didn't know what that meant, but I grabbed the phone as soon as she nodded. The clink, clink, clink of coins dropping into a pay phone meant Daddy was on the road.

"Hey, Sugar Bee," the voice said. "Know you just settled in but I miss you."

"Daddy!" I chewed on my lip when it started to quiver. His voice sounded a million miles away. Which he just about was.

Grandma Clark's phone didn't have an extra-long cord to drag into the hall closet. But I sure didn't want her to know hearing my daddy almost made me cry. Still, when he said our cat, Lulu, was fine and Mama said tell me it was hot as the dickens in Texas, I bit the inside of my cheek extra hard to keep from sniffling.

"Where are you?" I asked.

"Amarillo. Mama's at work. Sends her love. We better

hang up before I have to sell my truck to pay for this." I heard some clicks, then his voice. "Having trouble hearing you," he said.

But I had so many questions! What did Mama know about the beautiful painted plate upstairs in her room? Was it valuable? Should I tell Grandma Clark I'd broken it? Did they know actual Chinese people lived in Paris Junction, not to mention possible shoplifters?

His voice came back for a second. "Love you, Azalea."

"Daddy," I whispered. "When can I come home?" I glanced at Grandma Clark. The look on her face was pure hurt.

The line went dead while I was holding on. I hadn't asked whether we were going to the Grand Canyon or if my friend Barbara Jean had stopped by to ask if I was okay.

"I could hardly hear him. There were so many clicking noises."

"Probably the operator snooping." Grandma Clark frowned, shook her head. "Mavis could still be listening. She loves to tattle everybody's business all over town."

"Our telephones back home don't need operators. Nobody I know shares the same line." But mostly I thought, *Holy crow. It's 1952 already. This place needs new phones.*

I carefully put my grandmother's heavy black phone down, wishing even more I was back in Texas.

# Chapter 8

The next morning before the sun was up, I heard clanging around downstairs. "Azalea! Get moving, girl. Need you down here. I can't reach my big hat."

Yep, that was my grandmother.

I tumbled out of bed and pulled on yesterday's shorts and shirt. When I got to her room, Grandma Clark was dressing herself in working clothes and one old shoe, still cussing at the bandage on the other foot. "Hand me my clean apron. Today's the day you meet the helpers."

Oh, brother. They would probably make fun of me being named for a pink bush, wearing cowboy boots, or if I tripped on a root and fell flat on my face.

First garden helper to ring the doorbell was the prissiest-looking girl I ever laid eyes on. She waltzed in, sweeping her blond bangs to one side, straightening a bow as big as a basketball. I'm sure she puts her hair up in pin curls every single night. You will never catch my ponytail in pin curls. When she jangled a charm bracelet and flounced her skirt, you couldn't help noticing she had on shiny shoes with a little bit of a high heel. Dopiest things on earth to wear anywhere, especially a garden. Guess she didn't figure on pulling up actual weeds.

"Come right in, Melinda," my grandmother said.

This Melinda hugged the book she was carrying tighter than if it was *Pippi Longstocking*. Or a dog story I'd read a zillion times. But it wasn't. It had *Party Planning for Fun* scrolled across the front in fancy letters.

"Do you need help in the kitchen, Mrs. Clark?" the girl gushed. "I've been practicing my lemon pound cake."

She *practices* pound cake?

"Garden work today." Grandma Clark nodded at me to help her into the dining room. Melinda followed.

I tugged at the bottom of my mostly clean shirt to cover up a tiny tear in my shorts, smiling to be friendly like Mama says. But I might as well be a piece of chewed-up gum stuck to Melinda's fancy shoe.

So I sneaked back to the kitchen to watch the clock, wishing that stupid little cat tail would move faster and make this day disappear. The doorbell's buzz jolted me out of scheming to march over to the phone booth in front of Mr. Wong's store, call my daddy, and beg him to come save me.

When I opened the front door, the boy from the garden headed straight for my grandmother. He bowed a little and his straight black hair fell over his glasses. "Hello, Mrs. Clark. My great-aunt sent this. She hopes you feel better." He handed her a wrapped-up present and put his hand out. She beamed and shook it.

The Chinese boy in the tree, Billy Wong. What an apple polisher!

Grandma Clark tucked the gift to the side of her wheelchair. "Tell Mrs. Wong I appreciate it."

I didn't have time to disappear into the kitchen again before guess who was at the door. Looking like he'd rather walk barefoot on burning-hot tar than stand in my grandmother's front hall. I had to tell Grandma Clark quick! There was a possible thief in her house!

When she saw that boy, the corners of my grandmother's smile turned upside down. "Come on in, Willis."

Willis? The name Miss Jane Partridge, the lady with

the big pocketbook and the file folder, mentioned should be working off some crime?

The exact same crook Mr. Wong shooed out of his grocery store yesterday?

Willis? Standing between my grandmother's fragile figurines and Billy, Mr. Wong's very own kin. He somehow managed to stick his hand *and* his bottom lip out. Then, crossing his arms over his chest, he scowled a quick "Hey."

Holy moly mashed potatoes, this could get interesting.

"You all may not know each other, especially my granddaughter," Grandma Clark said when she caught her breath. "Azalea Morgan, meet Melinda Bowman, Willis DeLoach, and Billy Wong, my garden helpers."

I waited for them to snicker about my name. But Billy shook my hand and prisspot Melinda half smiled. We followed Grandma Clark to the back door. Shoving ahead, Willis kamikazed off the top step onto the ground. Oh, brother, what a show-off.

After I helped my grandmother into a backyard chair, I grabbed a bucket. But I never took my eyes off Willis, who probably had a plan to pocket the best rose clippers.

Grandma Clark straightened her sun hat and pointed up under the stairs. "Gardening gloves in that basket. Shovels and clippers over there, children."

From where I sat, there weren't any children in this garden. Willis could have whacked down her tallest tomato plant with one arm chop—*and* he was surely a shoplifter. Melinda was flouncing her skirt out, moseying around in ridiculous shoes. Billy's manners made him sound eighty, and I was almost twelve, sure as shooting not a child.

My grandmother kept giving orders. "Billy, you pick the last of my tomatoes. Plenty for your store." Her eyes cut over to Willis, who'd sneaked away to peer into her garden shed window and rattle the door handle. Grandma Clark called out, "Willis! Get over here!"

He sauntered back. "Yes, ma'am?" he said, all innocent-like.

"Nobody needs anything inside my shed. Stay out. All of you." She picked up her cane and shook it toward the side fence. "Even if you're only working today, Willis, you can pull up honeysuckle."

When Melinda opened her mouth like she was about to ask if she could get on inside and bake something, Grandma Clark said, "Green beans are finished. The bamboo poles can come out." Melinda's prissy smile disappeared quicker than her shoes sank into the soft dirt. Then my grandmother looked right at me and said, "Azalea, tend to the roses."

43

She's letting *me* touch her precious roses?

She reached into her apron pocket for her metal clippers, shining like she polished them every day. She opened and closed them carefully, showing me the sharp edge. "Take care. I promised Preacher Jones I'd send my prizewinning Climbing Iceberg beauties for a funeral tomorrow."

I leaned close enough to smell the roses' sweetness. I touched a stem, careful of the prickly thorns. Before I could cut a single rose, a million crushed petals fell into my hand. I jiggled another stem, pricked my finger, and dropped the clippers in a puddle of water.

I handed a few roses to Grandma Clark.

"Azalea," she said, eyebrows raised. "These will never do." She wiped her clippers on her apron and tossed my roses in the mulch heap. Real quick, I went back to pulling up weeds.

We'd pretty much attacked every dead thing in Grandma Clark's garden when she finally called out, "Leave the gloves and trowels next to Azalea."

I may not know how to clip her roses, but it looked like I was still the Number One Helper. I stacked buckets and put away gloves and tools till she took off her wide sun hat and fanned herself. "Show everybody out, Azalea," she said. "See you next week, children."

The thing was, I'd like to show them out and pray they *never* come back. Not next week, not ever. If I didn't like talking to new people before I got to Paris Junction, my mind had not changed today.

Here's what went wrong in the garden.

1. Willis *accidentally* sprayed Billy with the hose.
2. I may have ruined Grandma Clark's clippers.
3. A possible shoplifter worked side by side with the person he might have stolen from.

After Grandma Clark was settled inside, I opened the front door. Just in time to see Willis point to his own brown crew cut, then to Billy's straight black hair, making a face, mumbling the words *bad haircut*. He did something funny with his eyelids, pulling them up and down, mocking Billy.

Billy flinched, then jammed his fists in his pockets. I shot Willis my meanest look. He ignored me and whispered to Melinda, loud enough for me to hear, "Slanty Chinaman eyes." They snickered all the way down the sidewalk.

Billy left, too, in the other direction.

I was happy to be rid of those helpers, every last one of them.

"Grandma Clark, did you hear Willis making fun of Billy Wong?" I said when I pushed her wheelchair toward the kitchen.

She sat up straighter. "Can't have that. What did he say?"

"Showed off something awful. Said ugly things about his hair. Willis is mean!"

"I will not have that behavior in my house."

I plopped down on the chair closest to my grandmother. "And also? I think I saw Willis DeLoach shoplifting at Lucky Foods."

Grandma Clark's kitchen hardly had enough room for both of us, but she wheeled around quick. "Willis is not supposed to be at the Wongs' store. You saw him there? Stealing something?"

"Well, maybe."

"Tell the truth, Azalea. Don't create more problems by being untruthful." Grandma Clark leaned forward and took my hand. "If you're not sure, we don't need to get involved in the Wongs' business."

I answered as truthfully as I could. "Willis ran out of the grocery store yesterday like he had a firecracker in his shoe. And *maybe*, no, *probably*—there was a lot of stolen bubble gum in his pocket."

# Meanness

Willis DeLoach thinks he can hurt.

With his names, his jokes.

Chinaman.

Chink.

You eat rats?

I've heard all that.

Words bounce off me. I'm strong.

Strong as my sister May Lin's hands on piano keys.


May Lin tells me:

*Ignore them.*

*Walk away.*

A new school is for new things.

A club, a team.

Write for the newspaper.

Take trigonometry. Miss Jones's advanced English.

Make signs.

Make friends.

Make a promise.

Not to tell Great Uncle.

Not to tell May Lin.

Willis made me mad.

Mad enough to haul off and slug him.

Mad enough to yell.

Mad enough to call him a thief,

that he should be in jail.


Tonight, in the darkness,

my pillow catches my tears.

Where nobody but me can see.


*Billy Wong, Mad at the World*

# Chapter 9

By the time I'd cleaned up after the helpers, and Grandma Clark had finished shaking her head with worry over Willis and Billy, I was too hot to move.

My grandmother had other ideas. "Help me to my room and turn on the radio, Azalea. Go read a magazine on the porch where it's cool."

Cool, my foot. I could die of heatstroke sitting on the front steps. But just in time to save me from boredom, here came a man walking the world's littlest dog, barking her head off. Now, I love dogs more than anything. Cats, too. I'm a whole lot better at talking to animals I don't know than people I don't know. But this one looked plenty mad.

In case I was attacked by a dog not much bigger than a rat, I backed up. The man pulled on a skinny leash and waved real big, same as most everybody in Paris Junction.

"Afternoon. I'm Henry Jackson. This here's Tiny, my Chihuahua. I do some handiwork for your grandma. My bike and auto fix-it place is over past Main Street."

"I'm Azalea. Visiting from Texas."

"I know about you, Azalea. Even met you once or twice. Last time, when your mama and daddy brought you back for Mr. Clark's funeral. Showing you off to anybody who'd listen and look!" Mr. Jackson winked, then sat next to me on the steps. "Knew your mother when she was a girl. Your daddy, too, that crazy scoundrel. Yes, indeedy. I could spin a story or two, especially about little Mary Josephine."

"Mary Josephine? Everybody calls Mama JoBelle now," I said.

Oh boy. This is gonna be good. I could listen forever to Mr. Jackson talking and I wouldn't even have to say much.

"She changed a lot when she left here." He picked up his dog and I reached out to pet her. "Go ahead, she won't bite." Tiny looked at my fingers and I swear she turned her nose up. "Your parents coming soon, Azalea?" he asked.

"After Grandma Clark gets better. We were supposed to go to the Grand Canyon on vacation." I slammed shut my grandmother's dopey magazine for emphasis.

"Paris Junction's not the Grand Canyon, that's for sure. But maybe you'll enjoy us." Now he held Tiny so tight she'd stopped barking and frowning. But she *was* shaking every bone in her body. "Your grandmother's got some good help, right?"

"Never lived in a place where everybody helps so much."

"That's the nice thing! You'll see." Then his eyebrows went straight up in a question. "You like to ride a bike?"

Mr. Henry Jackson was about the easiest person in the universe to talk to. I took a big breath and let it out with what Mama calls a lot of drama. "Bike's back home in Texas. Won't be here long enough to need it."

"We'll see about that." He laughed and put Tiny down next to him, real close. "Your grandma resting?"

"Maybe. Want to come in?" I scooted up one step from his dog, who was now grinning. Or maybe baring her teeth at me.

"Miz Clark don't allow dogs inside. You got pets, Azalea?"

"A cat. Named for my favorite cartoon character, Little Lulu. Even though she's bigger than Tiny." Thinking about that made me laugh. "Daddy says we've moved around way too much to have a dog. But I love all animals."

"That's nice." Tiny started yapping again. "Hush, Tiny! You're liable to disturb most of Paris Junction." He calmed down his dog, then said, "Thought I'd get some work done on the shed out back today."

"The shed?" I stood up and quietly closed the front door. I was about to learn something good.

"Promised I'd give the place a fresh coat of paint, and the windows need ivy pulled away. Not like anybody goes in there no more." When Henry Jackson laughed, his hand went to his mouth, covering up a place where a tooth was missing near the back. But his bright brown eyes made it easy to smile with him.

"Willis DeLoach was here with the garden helpers this morning, snooping around the shed. Grandma Clark shooed him away." I kicked a little rock off the sidewalk with my sandal and followed Henry around back, two steps to every one of his big strides. "Grandma Clark claims spiders live in her shed."

He clamped his lips together, shook his head, then said, "Uh-huh. You don't say." Now Tiny was stretched out next to a tomato plant, chewing on a stick bigger than she was. When she stood up and growled, Henry pointed his finger, saying, "Tiny, sit." She kept dancing on her dainty little feet. "She's thinking about it." He laughed again and I did, too.

"I'm getting good at pulling weeds. Want me to help?"

"You can watch for now." He wiped his bald head with a red bandanna, then took out sharp garden shears and attacked the thick vines. "I imagine you're good for your grandma. Maybe better than Mary Josephine ever was."

"Mama sure didn't learn about growing flowers and vegetables from my grandmother."

Mr. Jackson swiped his bandanna across his head again, then started back clipping and talking. "Your mama wasn't one to sit still for long. She enjoyed her dancing. And going to a picture show with Johnny Morgan. Aggravated Mrs. Clark. Your grandmother's an artist, don't you know."

"My grandmother's an artist?"

"Used to be. Ask her about it."

Well, I'll be. Grandma Clark and I had one thing in common.

After Henry Jackson cleared most of the ivy off the windows, I tried to peek through a dirty pane. "What's in there? Besides spiders? My mama's old books or something? Wonder why Grandma Clark told us to stay away."

"Your grandmother has her own ideas about things, Azalea."

And that was all he said about that.

See if I cared about this falling-down old shed.

But I did care. Something about it was important to my grandmother. Grown-ups are always saying tell the truth. Then sometimes they up and tell bald-faced lies themselves. Grandma Clark claimed nothing was in there but bugs? I bet there was something more.

Mr. Jackson handed me Tiny's skinny red leash. "If you really want to help, Tiny might appreciate a walk down the street a little ways."

Okay, even if Tiny's not the friendliest dog in the universe, sooner or later, all dogs loved me. But I hardly got two houses away before a bike zoomed past and Willis DeLoach skidded to a stop. Of course, Tiny started barking again.

Willis backed up like he was worried he'd get his leg gnawed off. "Get that mutt away from me!"

I wanted to grab Tiny and run back to my grandmother's. I did *not* want to stand here on the sidewalk with Willis. But I picked up Tiny, willed my heart not to jump out of my shirt, and said as loud as I could, "If you weren't so mean to her, she'd be friendly." Though truthfully, so far she hadn't gotten *real* friendly even to me.

Willis took off his cap, and it was all I could do not to laugh at his smushed-down hair, his bright red ears. Puffing up his chest and looking down at me, he announced, "I can outrun a dog. I'm faster than anybody you know. But she's a barker. Probably bites, too." He shook his cap at Tiny and the dog yipped even louder. "You don't know whether she's a bad dog. You don't live in Paris Junction."

He peeled off on his bike, almost knocking me and Tiny off the sidewalk.

"Watch where you're going!" But my voice disappeared in the dust turned up by Willis's tires. Now Tiny was shaking like a big wind had blown through, and really and truly, so was I. "It's okay. You're safe now," I said.

When we walked into my grandmother's yard, Henry Jackson was packing up his tools. He held his shivering dog and looked her straight in the eye. "You okay, Miss Tiny?"

"Had to save her from Willis DeLoach and his bike. He's scary."

Mr. Jackson shook his head and muttered something about that boy not having the sense the Good Lord gave a tadpole, then nodded toward the garden shed. "Tell your grandma I'll be back the next cool day. Once school's started, I'll have time for painting. Lots of bikes need fixing before September!" He headed down the sidewalk, waving Tiny's little paw over his shoulder. "Thanks for the walk! And Azalea? You watch out for Willis. That boy's often up to no good."

"You can say that again." I turned up the sidewalk and I skipped over every crack. Willis DeLoach almost running me down with his bike was enough bad luck for one day.

# Chapter 10

WWhen Grandma Clark rolled her wheelchair into the kitchen, I was washing Willis cooties off my hands. With soap. You can't be too careful when it comes to standing close to somebody like Willis DeLoach.

I helped her into the living room and collapsed on the sofa. "Henry Jackson was here," I said. "I offered to pull honeysuckle and ivy off the shed. He didn't need me."

Grandma Clark reached for her sewing box. "Henry loves to talk."

"He told me you're an artist," I said quietly.

"Not these days. No time for that foolishness." She fluffed a faded blouse in the air, then settled it back on her lap. I thought about saying I was an artist, too, but she punched a needle through a button and snapped her mouth shut, like that was that.

A little fan turned slowly from side to side, blowing hot air around the living room. Leaning back onto the sofa to let the room's quietness settle around me, I remembered something. "Mama told me you like ice cream. I saw a sign in the drugstore window downtown. Said they have a soda fountain. Want to get some?"

Grandma Clark dropped her sewing and looked up. "Too hot to be pushing wheelchairs. Why don't *you* run downtown? Billy should be working at his great-uncle's grocery. If they can spare him, invite him for ice cream."

"Me? Get ice cream with Billy?" I shook in my boots thinking about it.

Grandma Clark nodded toward her coin purse on the table. "Can't think why not. Take enough money to treat."

*I* could think why not. Just because Willis was mean and I wanted to take up for Billy didn't mean I needed to talk to a Chinese boy and eat at the same time. But I liked ice cream a lot. I tucked my shirt into my shorts and grabbed two quarters.

And that's how I happened to be eating ice cream at

Ward's Drugstore and Soda Fountain, side by side with Billy Wong.

Now, Daddy always tells me focusing right at a person's eyes shows you're interested, no matter how hard it is. I slowly spun my stool around two times, then stared into Billy's eyeglasses. After I took a deep breath, I made myself ask, "How long have you lived in Paris Junction?"

Billy dipped an Oreo into his ice cream. "Two weeks," he said. "But I've visited. A lot. Everybody in my family lives here or across the river in Shallowater." He didn't seem to mind talking to a stranger he'd just met pulling up weeds. And he spoke perfect English, like me.

"You don't talk like you look." I licked my spoon and wondered if that sounded rude. "You ever live in China?"

He took polite nibbles at his cookie and answered, "Never even been to China. I was born in Mississippi. Where my parents have their grocery. This summer they sent me to live with my great-aunt and uncle so I could get ready for school. Seventh grade, starting soon."

"If I ever get back to Texas, I'll be in sixth grade." I scraped the last bite of my banana split and ignored the look from a waitress wearing a funny hat and a *Gloria* name tag. When Gloria pursed up her lips and started talking to the lady drinking coffee at the other end of the counter, the words *granddaughter* and *Mrs. Clark* and *Chinese boy* drifted my way. I put down my spoon and shifted on my stool. "What's she talking about over there?" I whispered.

Billy shrugged. "Maybe she thinks we shouldn't be sitting together at her drugstore. You and me."

Just when I was getting brave enough to talk to a complete stranger, somebody had to make me worry over what to say next.

"My mama claims you can't turn around twice here without somebody gossiping about what you ate for breakfast."

"Guess I didn't notice. Shallowater's a pretty small town, too," Billy said.

"I've lived in a bunch of places. If you don't count my second-grade teacher making us do an ancestor project, nobody ever cared about my family or what we were doing."

Billy didn't answer but Gloria sure slammed the check on the counter and squinted through her cat's-eye glasses at us. The little rhinestones in the corners caught the light over the soda fountain when she leaned close and said, "That's thirty cents. You're taking up space needed for the regulars."

I glanced at the empty stools, then slid my grand-mother's change across the lunch counter.

As we headed toward the door, Billy spotted a wire rack near the big front window. "Hold on, Azalea. I collect these comic books. Mostly *Superman*."

I turned the spinner around and reached in my shorts pocket. Two dimes. I could buy me and Billy a comic book. "My favorite's *Little Lulu*."

Billy didn't answer. His head was stuck inside *Superman*.

"No reading without paying," Gloria hollered from behind the counter. "Time for you two to go."

I put Lulu back where she belonged. I wasn't buying anything else from rude Gloria. I left Ward's Drugstore real quick and Billy followed.

"I better get back. Grandma Clark shouldn't stay by herself too long."

"I'll walk partway with you. If I hurry, Great Uncle won't mind. The store shouldn't be too busy till supper-time."

Maybe something about walking side by side made it easier to talk. But when this thought jumped out of my head and into my mouth, I said it out loud. "I saw Willis DeLoach at your grocery store. Mr. Wong didn't seem too happy."

61

Billy frowned. "He's not supposed to be there. They caught him shoplifting a couple of weeks ago and turned Willis over to a judge for punishment."

I took a sharp breath, considering whether to tell Billy that the judge was in cahoots with Miss Partridge. And *she's* the one who forced him on my grandmother. Or how I'd seen Willis with that bubble gum at Lucky Foods. Before I could decide, here came Willis and two boys with canasta cards clothespinned to their bike spokes, clicking and zooming up the street. One of them stopped, reached down for a fistful of gravel, and tossed it right next to me.

"Go back where you came from!" Willis yelled as they sped off.

Billy grabbed my hand, pulling me back, saving me. Once I caught my breath, my voice was shaking. "Why're they mad at me?"

"It's me Willis wants to leave Paris Junction," he answered quietly, kicking a stone off the sidewalk.

"Huh? What'd *you* do?"

"Nothing."

"Why's he so mad?"

"Maybe because Chinese are going to his white school now. For a long time, we had the Chinese Mission

School, where my sister and brother went. Chinese students came from all over the place. Some even lived there."

"How come you're not going? Like your brother and sister."

"The school closed. The rules changed. Now we're allowed to go to Paris Junction Junior High. In the same building with the high school."

Billy sounded like that was the best thing in the whole world, going to a big new school. I'd be shaking in my boots, walking the halls with high school seniors!

"You want to go to a whole school of people you don't know?"

"I play baseball with some of the white kids," he said. "And I plan to write for the *Tiger Times* school newspaper. Run track, join a few clubs. Even if Willis thinks I don't belong."

"Does he own the school?"

Billy shrugged, then laughed. "My sister says ignore Willis. Hard to ignore today, when he's throwing rocks."

The thought popped into my head that I'd been talking to Billy Wong all the way to my grandmother's house and I hadn't run out of things to say.

He turned back toward Main Street, then stopped. "Tell Mrs. Clark thanks for the ice cream," he said. "Oh, and, Azalea, you got a bike? We could ride together along the creek behind our store. You like to hunt turtles? Fish?"

If I hadn't already talked more than I'd talked in my entire lifetime to a boy, I'd be explaining that *no, I will not be exploring a creek.* I will be fixing dinner and watering Grandma Clark's garden till the cows come home. Or at least till my mama comes to take me home. I probably won't be riding any old bike, either, or fishing or catching turtles. Even though it was easy eating ice cream together, I had a hard time picturing being good friends with a boy. Especially one so different.

But today was fun. So I looked right at Billy Wong, and I answered, "Maybe."

# Notes for *Tiger Times* Report

Banana split: 20¢

Ice cream and cookie: 10¢

*Superman* comic: 10¢

Jimmy Olsen, cub reporter, is my hero.

If you read comics without buying,

the waitress will get you.

Chinese students not to sit at counter too long.

Especially with a white girl.

Even if she's your friend.


*Billy Wong, Reporting the Facts*

# Chapter 11

I t's nice you and Billy are becoming friends," Grandma Clark said when I opened the kitchen door.

Being friends with somebody other than Barbara Jean? Barbara Jean had announced to our entire class last year in Texas that she thought Azalea was the most interesting name she could imagine. She knew I was terrible at dodging and cracking but she'd picked me first for dodgeball and crack the whip. She'd hopped on the top row of the chorus risers when I was the only girl Miss Fife stuck up there. Just because I was the tallest girl in fifth grade, Barbara Jean said, didn't mean I had to stand with the boys.

And now I'd practically forgotten my best friend.

I pulled a wooden chair next to my grandmother, who was sitting with her foot propped on a stool. "Billy says thanks for treating. We talked about that school where his brother and sister went."

Only a tiny breeze floated in the window, and Grandma Clark fanned herself with the newspaper. "Before they closed the Chinese Mission School, my church helped with their big garden," she said. "His older sister and brother worked with me. I've known Billy's great-aunt since she joined our Women's Missionary Union."

A picture of the scary, frowning people hanging in her upstairs hallway popped into my head. My grandmother wasn't as scary as I'd thought she might be, though. So I asked, "We don't have a big family like Billy, do we? No aunts and uncles. Not a one."

"Families come in all shapes and sizes. JoBelle was plenty for your grandfather and me." Grandma Clark rolled her eyes and pressed her lips together like she was trying very hard to keep the words inside. Before I could ask another question, she reached for her toes with a back scratcher Mama had given her, and that was all she said about that.

"Time for supper. I managed to get the neighbor's meatloaf in the oven. Serve it up, Azalea."

Never mind that I'd eaten an entire banana split and I wasn't nearly hungry enough for supper. Or that she still wasn't saying please. I sliced tomatoes from the garden and only nicked myself once. Sticking my finger in my mouth, I held the pot holder with the other hand and grabbed the meatloaf. Grandma Clark didn't notice I was bleeding, but I didn't drop the meatloaf, either.

"While we're eating, turn on my kitchen radio."

"Yes, ma'am." I switched on the music, and she nodded in time to the songs.

Even though Daddy loved to spin Mama around, dancing everywhere, I'd never heard the old-timey music playing now. Then, the second I speared a tiny bite of meatloaf, a song came on that made me drop my fork.

"That's my mama's favorite!" I hummed along about a blue moon and a dream in my heart.

"The day I was born, Daddy called the radio station and requested that song for Mama and me."

My grandmother put down her iced-tea glass and settled her hands in her lap. "You don't say," she said very quietly.

"I know all the words. Since I was barely tall enough to put my arms around his waist, I've danced on my daddy's shoes." I was still a little mad at Mama, but remembering her and Daddy carrying on to music made me smile.

Grandma Clark turned to face the window, away from me. "Get me some more tea, Azalea. While you're up, cut off the radio."

"But I love 'Blue Moon.'"

"I asked you to turn it off. We've heard enough," she answered.

While I pushed a fat red tomato slice around my plate in the quiet of the kitchen, Grandma Clark finished her meatloaf. I wheeled her to her room and she leaned back on her pillow and closed her eyes. "I'm tired tonight. Run on up to your room. Enjoy yourself."

I stomped upstairs and flung myself across the bed. How was I supposed to *enjoy myself*? I didn't want to be here in the first place. The only person nice to me was probably off riding his bike and catching a fish. Me? I'm stuck in this little blue house, in dopey Arkansas. I opened the drawer and yanked out my sketchbook.

Uh-oh. That plate. I picked up the broken pieces and laid them on my bed. Would they ever fit back together? With the thick gold rim around the edges and the purple of the huge fairy wings, it sure looked like something special. I could never paint anything so beautiful. Mr. Jackson said my grandmother is an artist. Had Grandma Clark made this?

I needed to tell her it was broken. But if I did, I could be in trouble. If I didn't, I wasn't telling the truth. I hadn't known my grandmother long, but I knew how she felt about the truth.

Stuffing the pieces as far back in the drawer as I could, I stared at a blank sketchbook page. Back in Texas, I could draw my cat curled up on the sofa. I scribbled a few curlicued *A*s and *M*s, but my heart wasn't in fancy writing. Barbara Jean would say draw the clouds. She was partial to puffy clouds that looked like kittens. But what's there to draw here? Nothing, that's what.

Sitting up, I leaned on the windowsill and stared clear to the back fence. A rising moon reflected off the shed's blue door. Grandma Clark said mostly spiders lived in her garden shed and I'd better stay out. But maybe she'd forgotten. What if it was full of something else?

Like roller skates.

Old *Little Lulu* funny books.

My mama's diaries.

I'd seen Mr. Jackson hide the key on a hook. I waited till it got darker and Grandma Clark was surely asleep before tiptoeing downstairs, one creaky step at a time. I listened in front of her bedroom door. Quiet snoring. I crept along the walkway to the back fence. Lifting the key chain off the hook, careful not to drop it, I put the key into the lock. The door was hard to push, stuck almost, but it opened.

A flashlight was next to the door. I held my breath and danced the light across a little bed squished between two tables. One table was crowded with boxes of nails and hooks and thumbtacks. A stack of dusty books was on the other. I sat in the desk chair and twirled it around once, shining the flashlight around the room. In the corner was an open door. To a bathroom, with a commode. Had somebody ever lived in here?

I turned slowly around again. Wow. A long shelf filled with rows and rows of teacups and saucers and plates. Like the one I'd broken! They were so perfect I could almost smell the flower decorations. Should I ask my grandmother about the easel and the canvases propped against the back window? But I couldn't admit I'd sneaked into a place she told me—and all her garden helpers—to stay away from. I turned a cup over, careful not to break it, and looked on the bottom. The initials were A.A.C. Were they Grandma Clark's? I put the cup back where it belonged.

Before my grandmother woke up and hobbled into the garden to holler at me, I reached for the key I'd set next to a glass perfume bottle painted with flowers. I stopped and sprayed the bottle twice. Nothing but hot, dusty air. I took a deep breath. What this room really smelled like was turpentine, old books, and secrets.

Shaking off the shivers, I tiptoed down the path and into my room. I opened the drawer to hide my sketchbook next to the broken plate. I whispered the words written on the cover. *Keep Out. Private. This Means You.*

# Chapter 12

A few days after I'd sneaked into the shed, it rained. Hard. But by the time the garden helpers came back, the sun was beating down. We pulled weeds and swatted at sweat bees till my grandmother finally said come sit under the tree. She'd made lemonade. Make that her Number One Helper had made the lemonade. Me.

Maybe she was trying to get Willis DeLoach to stop making fun of Billy. Because for some reason, she was going on about being polite and minding your manners. Melinda sat closest to Grandma Clark. Billy smiled nicely. Willis had showed up late, missed most of the weeding. When he slipped into his seat at the picnic table, it was in time to hear Grandma Clark say, "It's common courtesy to remember names. And to look a person right in the eye when you meet them."

My least favorite thing is looking right in somebody's eyes.

Grandma Clark wasn't finished. "If you're shy about that, focus on their forehead."

Willis jerked his head around every which way. "You mean like those ugly cyclops things, with an eye in the middle of their head?"

That boy gets on my last nerve.

Grandma Clark ignored him. "To remember a person's name, make up something to relate it to."

Well, I could do that!

Willis DeLoach—Worst Roach.

Melinda Bowman—Bossy Bow.

After my grandmother finished our Good Manners lesson, she sent the helpers back to weeding. She sent me inside. "Wash out the lemonade pitcher, Azalea," Grandma Clark said.

I tromped in the back door and looked straight through to the front hall. Where I was sidetracked by a little girl sitting on the steps, singing to a loved-on baby doll.

"Hey there. Are you lost?" I asked.

She shook her head, and her lopsided ponytails zipped from side to side.

"Looking for somebody?"

"My brother's Willis," she whispered. Her eyes got big and she slowly spread the words out. "He's doing important work at this house."

Willis's sister thinks he's doing important work? Punishment for shoplifting's more like it. "I'm Azalea. He's in my grandmother's garden."

"My name's Lizzie. I'm almost five. We have a puppy in the pecan grove."

Holy moly, Willis had a puppy? Henry Jackson's dog, Tiny, sure didn't take to him.

"In the pecan grove?"

Lizzie tucked her plaid skirt around that doll like a blanket. "Where we live. But I'm not supposed to blab. If I don't tell, Willis gives me bubble gum." The girl put her finger to her lips. "Shh. Especially the part about the new puppy. Mama doesn't know. She's sick."

Before I could tell her I'd like to see a new puppy. And how much better I'd be at playing with puppies than talking to my grandmother's helpers. Before I could think of what to say to make her feel better about her mama, everybody poured out the front door, tracking thick mud onto the porch.

Melinda skipped down the steps in her pointy shoes, waving across the street to a girl stepping out of a car bigger than my daddy's truck. The girl ran up, squealing and cackling like a hen. They made me sick.

Then prisspot Melinda grabbed her friend's hand, whispered and giggled some more. "Nice skirt," she said to Lizzie.

"Yeah, nice plaid skirt," the other girl said. "Looks real familiar, doesn't it, Melinda?"

Willis stormed down the steps and took his sister's hand, brushing by those mean girls.

My grandmother called from behind the front screen door. "What's all this racket about?"

"We're leaving," Willis muttered, and he marched Lizzie down the sidewalk.

Melinda flicked a piece of dirt off her dopey shoes. "Thank you for the lemonade, Mrs. Clark," she sang out as she wobbled off with her friend. I wanted to trip her, see how that hair bow looked squished up against the sidewalk.

After Billy thanked my grandmother, he left faster than I could say *See you around*. Guess I still have a few things to figure out about talking to strange boys. My grandmother tapped both sides of her wheelchair lightly. "More than enough for today."

I pushed her into the living room and said, "That little girl Lizzie seems sweet. But Melinda and her friend were making fun of her clothes. What did they think was so funny?"

"I suspect it had something to do with the child's skirt. Which possibly came from the church resale shop. And previously belonged to one of them."

One more reason for me not to care a bit if Bossy Bow Melinda is a friend of mine.

"Daddy taught me to try to see everybody's true heart before you stare at their clothes or their hair or anything else."

Grandma Clark wrinkled her nose up like she wasn't sure who I was talking about. "I suspect Lizzie and Willis have been struggling. Their mother's not well. Mr. DeLoach does his best, but managing a pecan grove is hard work. Raising two children out there can't be easy."

Two children *and* a puppy, I didn't say.

My grandmother made an exasperated clicking sound. "Look at this. Front hall's a mess."

I was worn out from listening to so many people today,

but I grabbed the carpet sweeper and attacked the mud. "Guess nobody paid attention to your request: *Keep the place tidy. Wipe your feet on the way in.*"

"Next time, Azalea, have them come around the side of the house."

I don't even like talking to Melinda. Or Willis, for that matter. And I'm supposed to enforce her rules?

Grandma Clark took a breath as big as Texas. She sank back in her wheelchair and looked again at the hall carpet. "I swear, these garden helpers are almost more trouble than they're worth."

"You can say that again," I mumbled, and a smile flickered across her face. Some days, if I tried hard enough, I could almost see my grandma and me being friends.

# Chapter 13

"When you finish sweeping, pack up the leftover cookies," Grandma Clark said. "I owe Henry Jackson for his work. Turn at the library. His place of business is a little ways off Main Street."

"Yes, ma'am. And Grandma Clark? Your foot may be healing, but I bet your doctor doesn't want you jitterbugging or pulling up weeds while I'm gone."

Without smiling even a little, she left the cookies and the money on the dining room table and wheeled herself toward her bedroom. I hurried with the sweeper, hoping she wouldn't notice a few clumps of mud left on the carpet, then went looking for Mr. Jackson.

The minute I turned onto Main Street, a bike wheeled out from behind a tree and I jumped a mile. "Yikes, Billy. You almost made me drop these cookies."

"Sorry, Azalea." He hopped off his bike, straightened his glasses up on his nose, and smiled. "I'm making a delivery for the store."

I looked past the library, where a road veered off. "I'm taking cookies to Mr. Jackson's."

"Heading that way, too. Our store's not busy. Great Uncle won't mind if I'm a little late." Billy pushed his bike and I walked beside him. Side by side, together but not saying a word. The way I like it.

By the time we dropped off the Lucky Foods grocery delivery, a prickly heat rash had formed on my neck and sweat was pouring down my back. Finally, Billy parked his bike in front of the sign *Henry Jackson, Mechanic and Fixer-Upper*.

"Hey, anybody here?" I called out. Nobody answered but Tiny, yapping her head off. "It's Azalea. And my friend Billy."

Mr. Jackson stepped out from the back of his garage, wiping his hands on a greasy rag. "Afternoon, Azalea. Nice to see you, Billy." He wagged a finger at his dog to shush her.

I held the bag up. "Hope they aren't in a million crumbs."

He put the money in a cigar box with a tight rubber band around it. After he offered us a cookie and popped one in his own mouth, a grin started at one ear and spread clear to the other. "Mrs. Clark sure knows how to cook." He closed up the bag and nodded for us to follow. "Got something to show you, Azalea. Careful where you step." Mr. Jackson pointed to the stubby root of a weed tree, half buried in the dirt. "Been like that a while, root holding the door open, tree offering shade. Good for business having everybody walk right in."

I miraculously managed not to stumble. We scooted around a barrel of black floppy inner tubes inside the garage. Shelves were piled high with doodads I didn't recognize. When we got to the backyard, a blue bike was propped up on its kickstand.

"I was coming by your house tomorrow, and here you are. How 'bout that."

I looked at Mr. Jackson, then at the bike.

"Noticed Billy delivering groceries on his bike. Saw you two were becoming friends. So I fixed it up. It's what I do when I think folks need getting around town. Take old bikes, make 'em good as new!" Mr. Jackson wiped a spot off the fender, then rolled it toward me.

"Really? This is mine? Looks better than my old bike back in Texas."

Billy touched the soap-bubble-shaped circles decorating the fenders. "Now we can ride down to the creek to fish, catch some frogs together."

I don't know about frogs, but we sure could get away from Willis faster.

Mr. Jackson squeezed the tires. "Plenty of air. Try it out."

"Thanks, Mr. Jackson!" I hollered as I carefully put one foot on the pedal, grabbed the handlebars, and rode down the alley. "Holy moly, this thing is fast! Hope I don't crash and crack my head open!"

When I put on the brakes, he said, "I'll adjust it for you, girl." He tinkered with my bike seat till we heard a loud banging on the side of the garage. Whack! Whack! Whack! Tiny came yipping and yapping to Mr. Jackson. He scooped her up while I stepped behind Billy and covered up my ears.

And in strutted Willis DeLoach, big as you please. Lizzie was with him, smiling at Tiny and maybe at me. Willis's bike already went so fast, he'd nearly run me down twice. What was *he* doing here? I inched closer to Billy, who didn't flinch from Willis's scowling face.

"Need something, son?" Mr. Jackson asked.

"Tire's flat." Willis whipped his head toward the sidewalk. He glared at me and Billy. "Why're *you* here?"

Willis looked like a coyote about to pounce. But I took three deep breaths to keep my heart from jumping out of my chest and made my voice as loud as I could. "None of your beeswax," I answered.

Mr. Jackson stepped in front of me and Billy. "Bring your bike this way," he said.

While Willis wheeled his bike around back, Lizzie sat on the shady steps and took two little paper dolls out of her pocket. "Hey, Azalea. I remember you. Wanna play? This is the baby and that's her mama. Back at our trailer, I got lots more. Willis helped me make a dollhouse out of a shoe box."

I was having a hard time picturing Willis being helpful to anybody without a judge's orders. "Your brother plays with paper dolls?"

"Yep. Turned Lady's water bowl into a swimming pool, too. I left it at home. For Lady."

"Lady? Who's Lady?"

Lizzie whispered her answer. "Remember? The puppy I'm not supposed to tell about."

"I love animals. Especially puppies."

"Cutest puppy in the whole wide world. You can come see her." She unwrapped a piece of bubble gum and held it up. "Want to share? I got it for not being scared."

I was thinking of what to say when Willis stepped around the corner. "Don't talk to my sister," he said. He glared at Billy, then he grabbed Lizzie and her paper dolls. Before he pedaled down the street balancing his sister on his handlebars, he turned, sneered, then blew a gigantic bubble. Daring me to tell on him.

Pretty soon, Mr. Jackson came out, shaking his head.

"Why didn't he fix his own flat tire?" Billy asked.

"That boy doesn't know the difference between a bike chain and a piece of macaroni."

"So we might could let all the air out of a tire and Willis couldn't fix it to save his fanny?" I asked, mostly kidding.

Mr. Jackson laughed. "Now, Azalea. You behave yourself. Just 'cause Willis is up to no good, doesn't mean you should be. Boy don't have a lick of manners."

Billy walked toward his own bike and I pushed my new one right up behind him.

"Where're you young'uns off to?" Mr. Jackson asked.

"Maybe over to the creek?" Billy answered.

But I was hatching a plan for a better bike ride. If we hurried, we might not even have to talk to anybody. "Mr. Jackson, did you know there's a pecan grove outside of town?"

Henry Jackson's a lot like my daddy. Both of them love to tell a good story. So in no time flat, I'd learned the best time of year to pick up pecans and how much they cost last winter. I knew how far away the pecan grove was and exactly how to get there.

All I needed was to talk Billy Wong into coming along.

# Chapter 14

Another rainstorm early this morning had turned the dirt ruts into mud puddles and my new bike was a mess. But mud washes off. Puppies don't stay little forever.

"Wait up, Azalea! Creek's the other way!" Billy hollered over the rattle of his bicycle basket. When he stopped at the V in the road, his bike was facing the wrong direction. If I told him the truth, he might take off and leave. Honest to goodness, I had to keep up a conversation inside my head to be brave enough to go myself.

"Want me to show you where the creek comes out?" Billy asked.

"I have another idea. Mr. Jackson says to turn left here."

He looked to where the road disappeared into a big pecan grove, way back off the road. "Left? Where're we going? Thought you wanted to learn how to fish."

"Maybe later." Though I wasn't sure about baiting a hook with a real live worm. "I have an idea. It'll be fun." I pedaled hard, twisting and turning between tall trees, and Billy followed me. When we stopped, I said, "We'd better walk our bikes now. Quiet."

"Azalea, are we trespassing?"

"I don't think so."

"Why're we here in the middle of these trees? In the mud." Billy started to leave. I grabbed hold of his handlebars and didn't let go.

"Willis's sister says they have a new puppy. Don't you love puppies?"

For a few minutes, the only sound was loud black crows fighting way up on a tree branch. Billy finally looked at me and frowned. "Willis lives out here? My family doesn't want me to associate with Willis."

"He's probably not even home yet. We're just looking for the puppy. Not associating."

Billy took slow, deep breaths. He didn't move. "I've

never ridden this far out of town. Great Uncle won't like it if I ruin my bike. Or Willis ruins it. I need my bike for delivering groceries."

Really and truly, I didn't want to ruin *my* bike, either. I didn't even want to talk to Willis. It was taking a whole lot of nerve I didn't know I had to ride my bike this far. "We'll see the puppy and leave. Promise."

By the time we got to the end of the road, the sun had broken through the wet trees, making the green leaves sparkle. I pointed to a glint of white metal. "What's that?"

We moved closer and Billy stooped down behind a big tree. Almost like he wanted to disappear into the rough bark. "It's an old trailer, and the window looks cracked. Does anybody live here? Are you getting us in trouble?"

I wasn't used to trouble any more than I was used to talking to people I didn't know. But I was sure this was where the puppy lived. We'd look and leave.

Next to the tree where Billy was hiding, a full mailbox was half-open. I reached around to open it the rest of the way. Billy jammed it shut. "It's against the law to tamper with somebody's mailbox," he whispered. "Let's get out of here."

"Just a minute." Peeping from behind the tree again, I saw a shadow up under the trailer. I moved closer, stumbled over a rock, and banged my knee. Just when Lizzie opened the front door.

Uh-oh. Somebody *was* home. Standing up tall, I took a deep breath. "Hey there, Lizzie. That your puppy under the trailer?"

She hopped down from the front stoop and leaned over. "That's Lady! We found her all by herself and scared. We're taking care of her till Mama's home from the hospital. Mama loves animals. She's gonna be so excited."

Their mama's in the hospital? Maybe that's why the mail's overflowing.

Before I could get closer, guess who came charging around the corner. Willis, carrying a huge laundry basket and making a face like he'd swallowed a fried worm.

Oh, brother. Willis had seen us. Now what?

But wait a minute. Was Willis DeLoach doing his own laundry? Hanging towels and underwear on the clothesline? Exactly like I had to do at my grandma's?

Billy scooted next to me. "We should leave," he whispered, aggravated at me for sure.

But I wanted to pet that puppy.

Willis dropped his clean clothes and kind of kicked at the basket, shoving it under a scraggly bush. He gave me the meanest stare and shot his sister one, too. "Get over here, Lizzie," he said.

Lizzie ignored him and patted the ground to get Lady out from under the trailer. "You got a pet, Azalea?" she called out. "Does your grandma?"

The sight of Willis storming up with that big laundry basket was taken over by a vision of a puppy in the middle of my grandmother's knickknacks. "No pets here in Paris Junction," I said, slowly moving toward hers.

Willis marched over to a rickety old picnic table and picked up a bowl, then slammed it down. He flung the mushy cereal on the tree right next to Billy. I jumped a mile. Taking a few steps toward us, he said, mean as everything, "Get off my property. Nobody invited you."

Billy looked hard at Willis. "Your sister invited Azalea. Or we wouldn't be here." His voice got softer. "But maybe we can help. I could ask my great-uncle to change his mind about letting you shop at our store. Since your mom's not here."

Billy Wong was about the nicest boy in the universe.

Willis didn't agree. "We ain't no charity case. Don't need help and don't need anybody snooping. That's trespassing." Willis stuck his face too close to us and shot his fists straight up.

Lady was lying on the ground right next to Lizzie now, a squiggly ball of white fur. When I backed away from Willis, Lizzie said quietly, "My brother's mad 'cause I'm scared at night. He promised he's found us a place to go. A sleeping place."

I didn't know what Willis had up his sleeve, but he shot her a look that said *keep quiet*. Then he hissed at Billy in the meanest voice ever, "I see your squinty eyes over there, watching my dog. I said leave. Now."

"Shut up, Willis!" Even though I'd always promised Daddy never to say that, I had to take up for my friend. "Billy was trying to be nice."

I'd come to see the new puppy. That was all. I didn't want anything to do with Willis, now or ever.

I glanced back only once as we walked toward our bikes. As awful as Willis was to Mr. Jackson's dog, Tiny? As awful as he was to Billy? You'd think no animal and no person would want to get close to him. But there he was, sitting next to Lady, rubbing her belly. Lizzie was smiling. Willis smiled right back at her.

Billy left faster and madder than I'd ever seen him, and I hurried to catch up. Mud splashed on my legs, and now the mosquito bites on my arms had turned into bright red welts. But I couldn't get away fast enough. No matter how nice he treated his sister and her puppy, I didn't trust Willis DeLoach. I never should have brought Billy out here. I knew that now.

All the way to the edge of the pecan trees, Billy didn't talk. But when we stopped at Main Street, his words spilled out. "My bike's a mess. Willis is mad. Shouldn't have gone to their place, Azalea." And off he went, his long skinny legs pedaling fast. Whatever he said next disappeared into the wind without giving me a chance to answer.

Here I was sure I had a new friend, and I'd gone and made him mad. All because of a puppy and the meanest boy on the planet. I had a lot to learn about making friends.

## Letter Not Sent to the
## Paris Junction Newspaper

To Whom It May Concern:

On Saturday, August 9, 1952, Billy Wong, age
almost thirteen, and Azalea Morgan, age eleven,
attempted to visit the pecan grove where the
DeLoach family resides. Azalea had received news
that a young puppy named Lady had come to the
family's trailer. When Billy and Azalea arrived, Willis
threatened them. Although his sister invited them
to play with her pet, Willis yelled hurtful names.
And threw things.

   Mail at the house is not being read.

   The children are in charge of food and laundry.

   The parents, Mr. and Mrs. DeLoach, are not in
residence.

   Authorities should check on this.

   Willis DeLoach has broken the law before.

Billy Wong and Azalea Morgan fled the pecan
grove, riding their bikes as fast as the wind.

No one can know I was there.

*Billy Wong*
*Trespasser, Writing Anonymously*

# Chapter 15

Clutching my handlebars to stay balanced, I fought the wind in my face all the way to Ruby Street. Once I hosed off my bike and propped it against the tree, I took the steps two at a time.

"Azalea! You're louder than a herd of wild buffalo. When I was coming up, girls knew how to behave." Grandma Clark spun around in her wheelchair, looked at my muddy cowboy boots, and gasped. "Where *have* you been?"

I kicked off my boots and caught my breath. "Riding my bike with Billy" was all I was confessing to.

She adjusted her glasses to look out the window, then sniffed in a quick breath through her nose. "Your what?"

"Mr. Jackson fixes up bikes for people. Good as brand-new. He gave it to me." I wasn't admitting Billy and I had trespassed in a pecan grove and discovered Willis and Lizzie living all by themselves. Grandma Clark knew Mr. Wong had warned Willis to stay out of his store. But Lizzie and Willis must be hungry and scared out there. Except for Willis, did Lizzie have anybody, even a bossy grandmother, looking after her?

"I hope you aren't going to ride all over town, getting into trouble."

"No, ma'am."

If I was better at figuring out what to say to people, maybe I'd have a good answer for my grandmother. Maybe I'd know whether to tell her where I'd been, what we'd seen. But I wasn't used to getting in trouble any more than I was used to talking back to boys like Willis DeLoach.

Grandma Clark jabbed at a bobby pin holding her gray bun neatly together. She was still staring at my new bike outside the window. "You need to give it back. If you want a bike, I'll buy it."

"It's not forever. More like a loan for as long as I'm in Paris Junction." Yesterday I might have asked *How much longer do you think that will be?* Today all I could think about was Billy being mad and Lizzie being scared. "Please let me keep it. Billy wants me to ride down to the creek behind their store."

Of course, if I didn't figure a way to make up with Billy, I might never hunt frogs at that creek.

Grandma Clark smoothed the cotton apron over her lap. "I'm happy you and Billy are finding things to do. But if we keep this bike, you must be responsible, take care of it."

First of all, *we* won't be keeping the bike. It's mine. Then, as if she'd seen the picture in my head of her riding a bike, Grandma Clark said, "Doc Wiggins stopped by. Says as long as I've got you here, I can give this up." She slapped her hands against the sides of the wheelchair. Twice. "Get my cane. I can stand on two feet and wear both shoes. Never needed this thing in the first place."

Holy moly. I had no answer for that.

But I handed her the cane and watched her wobble around the kitchen before she collapsed into a chair. "Enough of this foolishness," she said. "It's past my suppertime."

So that's why she was grumpy.

I opened the icebox. Half-eaten casseroles. Milk. One apple. Four eggs and a wedge of cheese. Something inside the little freezer, wrapped up and hard as a brickbat. Supper didn't look too promising from this side of the icebox door.

Grandma Clark waited at the table while the cat clock

on her wall moved so slow I was sure it was broken. But no, that tail was still swinging. Tick-tock, tick-tock, back and forth.

"Fry me an egg," she said. "And I don't like eggs cooked in bacon fat."

"Don't know how to fry eggs. But I can make grilled cheese in butter. Daddy's a champ at grilled cheese."

"Glad to know he's good for something," Grandma Clark muttered. "Your mother mistakenly thought Johnny Morgan hung the moon and the stars."

"Daddy's good at a lot of things. He can sing and play the ukulele. Bet you didn't know that." I slammed the icebox door, then buttered the bread, just so.

"That reminds me. A package came yesterday." She pointed to a square box mostly hidden behind a neighbor's cake carrier. "Mr. Prentiss from the post office stopped by. Said it was too heavy for you to manage by yourself."

That's the thing about Paris Junction. Everybody knows I'm here helping my grandmother, and they decide what I can carry three blocks. I looked at the return address. Our house in Texas. Okay, now I was mad. "This came yesterday?"

I almost asked *You're just now telling me?* Instead I bit my lip hard when Mama's voice popped in my head, saying

*Be polite, Azalea.* Truthfully, right this minute, it wasn't so easy being polite.

Grandma Clark leaned toward my package. I could tell she was dying to see inside.

"Well, are you going to open it?"

"When I finish making supper." I didn't talk while I flipped our sandwiches, letting the cheese ooze out like Daddy taught me.

When Grandma Clark asked me to turn on the radio, I did.

When she asked how Billy was, I said fine.

When she asked how I liked my new bike, I answered with a smirk.

As soon as the plates were washed, my so-called grandmother was in her room with her sewing basket in her lap. I snatched that present and stormed upstairs, rattling the pictures of all my dead relatives. So what if she thought door slamming was impolite. She was probably too deaf to hear. My grandmother acted like she hadn't told me I had to give my new bike back to Henry Jackson. Or made me cook her supper. Or kept Daddy's package a secret for an entire day. All she wanted was somebody—anybody!—helping her all the livelong day. She didn't give a hoot whether it was me or a girl who practiced baking and flounced her hair. Like Daddy said, Grandma Clark could boss the legs off a chicken without ever saying please.

As I opened the package, I thought about how Grandma Clark was up and walking on her own. And soon I'd be leaving Paris Junction and never coming back. I wouldn't miss a soul. Well, maybe Billy Wong. But everybody else was nothing but mean. I peeled back the last tissue paper and a heavy glass paperweight slipped out. I read the note in my mama's handwriting three times.

*Miss You, Azalea. Love, Mama and Daddy*

Holding the paperweight tight, I flung myself across the bed. Was this from the Grand Canyon? Was Daddy there without me? Why had Mama signed the card? I should be at the Grand Canyon! My grandmother didn't need me. She didn't even *like* me.

Then I remembered what Daddy says. *Don't let the other feller get you down!* I threw some water on my face and marched downstairs. A spider skittered across the banister, making me jump and catch my breath. But I smushed the spider and stomped out the front door. So what if Grandma Clark's fragile knickknacks rattled.

Who cared.

# Chapter 16

Sitting on the porch steps, waiting for the sun to disappear behind the neighbor's house across the street, I clutched my paperweight. Truthfully, I was pretty mad at Daddy for sending a gift—maybe from the Grand Canyon—without a word of explanation. I was mad at Grandma Clark for a whole bunch of reasons. And I was worried Billy might give up being my friend. But when mosquitoes started to gnaw my arm off, I gave up frowning and tiptoed inside.

By the time I helped my grandmother to bed and parked her cane close by, I was tired from pretending to be nice. I trudged upstairs and opened my sketchbook, trying hard to ignore the broken plate beside it. But I still couldn't think of a single thing to draw. I doodled circles like the ones decorating my bike fender and stared out the window at the stars.

Just as I was giving up being mad at everybody, just as I was about to fall asleep in my dark room, I heard something outside my window. The voice got louder. "Azalea!" Was that my grandmother? Grabbing a shirt to wear over my shorty pajamas, I raced downstairs.

The kitchen light was on. The door open. But I didn't see anybody anywhere. I hurried outside, calling "Grandma Clark!" over and over till my heart's pounding drowned out the words.

I found my grandmother sitting on the walk, rubbing her arm. Her cane had rolled away.

"I must have tripped on a rock," she said quietly.

I knelt beside her, trying to get the words out. Through her thin nightgown, she was trembling, and I put my arm around her shoulder. "You walked down the steps by yourself?"

"Thought I saw a light in the shed."

I glanced up just as a dim shadow flickered across the window. I didn't know whether to run inside to call the police or keep my arm around Grandma Clark right here. Then the shed door opened, just a sliver. And somebody leaned out, holding a hoe like he was about to chop somebody else's head off.

Good gravy. Willis DeLoach? In my grandmother's backyard?

He ducked inside as quick as he'd popped out. Even though it was dark, I shot him a look, mad as everything. Grandma Clark stood up and wobbled toward the house. She held my arm tight and stared straight ahead.

My words squeaked out. "I'm calling the doctor." After I told the operator to get Dr. Wiggins to our house quick, I grabbed the metal ice tray from the freezer and rattled out some cubes. I tied the ice inside a dish towel like Daddy did when I turned my ankle funny.

"Careful you don't get that all over my floor. And get me a drink of water." Grandma Clark winced but I held the ice close to her arm. We both shivered like a wind had blown through the kitchen.

By the time she'd finished sipping her water, Dr. Wiggins had hurried from one street over. He bundled her arm to her chest with a big head scarf. "First thing in the morning, come to the clinic for an X-ray, Mrs. Clark. Think it's only a bad sprain. Better safe than sorry." He put two pills in her hand, clicked shut his black bag, and left as quick as he'd come.

When I settled my grandmother into her bed, she reached for my hand and whispered, "I saw a light in that garden shed. Call the police, Azalea."

"Nobody's out there, Grandma Clark." Inside my head, I crossed my fingers at telling that fib. But I didn't want to worry her. Biting my lip hard, I tucked the sheet around her and tiptoed into the kitchen.

And there was Willis DeLoach with his forehead pressed against the screen door, looking straight in. After I'd gotten my voice back, I stood close to him and whispered, "What were you doing? Spying? Trying to steal something?"

I slipped outside onto the step next to Willis. He kicked a rock off the walk and didn't answer.

"Maybe I'd better get Dr. Wiggins back. Or the police. Talk fast. Once that nosy telephone operator spreads the word, half the town will be lined up at our door with tuna casseroles and questions."

"I saw the shed and the hidden key when we worked out here," he finally said. "Daddy's gone to look after our mama."

"You're staying all by yourself way out in the pecan grove? No mama and daddy?"

"I'm almost fourteen. Old enough. But Lizzie was scared at the trailer."

"So you and Lizzie are both here? Oh, brother. Grandma Clark will skin me alive when she finds out you're in her garden shed full of breakable treasures and I didn't tell her."

"Sorry." Not a lot of meanness was left in Willis's voice now. "I saw that bed through the window. Mrs. Clark's always helping people. Thought she wouldn't care."

What had I said to make Willis think he could help himself to my grandmother's garden shed?

"Are you making a mess?"

"No. We're sleeping." A little meanness crept back into his words. "You can't make us leave. You aren't the boss of this garden." Willis turned and walked back to the shed.

"Right this minute, I *am* the boss of this garden," I said into the darkness.

But I couldn't make them leave in the middle of the night and I didn't feel like arguing when Grandma Clark might be inside falling out of her bed. Or calling out my name, needing more water. I tiptoed inside, thinking about how my grandmother was helpful to most everybody. She wouldn't want them out in that pecan grove, scared to pieces. I could picture Grandma Clark taking them in.

Maybe I'd drop a hint or two.

Then I remembered how hateful Willis was to Billy. How Miss Partridge claimed he'd stolen from Mr. Wong. What I'd seen that day at Lucky Foods.

And I added in my head, *Maybe I won't.*

# Chapter 17

For the first two minutes after I woke up the next morning, I believed I'd dreamed everything. Then Dr. Wiggins X-rayed my grandmother's arm. Told her not to budge all day. And I knew it was real.

Pushing Grandma Clark's wheelchair home from his clinic, I was shaking so hard I worried about falling flat on my face on the cracked sidewalk. What if she found Willis and Lizzie hiding in her garden shed? Sleeping all night in a place she told us to stay away from. And I hadn't told the truth.

Once my grandmother was resting, I put on a fake brave smile and said, "I'm in charge now. I'm taking over." But truly, the last thing I wanted to be was in charge of anything.

She twisted the bedsheets back and forth between the fingers of her good hand. "Don't be such a worrywart, dear. It's a sprain. I'll be better soon."

It sounded like she was trying to make herself believe it.

"Yes, ma'am," I answered.

Sitting with the knobby bedspread's bumps pressing on my sweaty legs, I smoothed out her pillow. Grandma Clark fiddled with her sheets again, then closed her eyes. "Thank you, Azalea," she whispered.

I might faint across her bed hearing those three words.

Instead, I slipped into the hall and picked up the phone. "Reverse the charges," I said when the operator asked me what I needed. I wasn't about to say to the nosy telephone lady what I really needed: somebody to help. Mama to tell me what to do.

I let it ring a thousand times before I placed the heavy black phone back on its cradle. I pictured Lulu sprawled on her favorite chair, listening. The thing is, my cat can't talk. Nobody was at my house in Texas to help. So I did what my grandmother would do if she wasn't in bed with a sprained arm. I walked outside, took the key off the hook, and checked the shed for damages. The bed was neatly made up. The chair was under the desk, the teacups and plates undisturbed, lined up perfectly. Willis and his sister were gone, and you'd never know they'd been there. Except that *I* knew.

Sitting under the tree outside, I tossed a hard green tomato up and down. Up and down. Worrying about everything under the sun. But before I had time to figure out where Willis and Lizzie would sleep tonight or whether I'd be in Paris Junction till Halloween, Billy opened the back gate.

I didn't know what to say. But after he handed me a whole cooked chicken and yesterday's Little Rock newspaper, Billy talked first. "Dr. Wiggins came in the store early this morning. My great-aunt sent this. You're my last delivery. I can stay awhile."

"Did you get in trouble? About your bike?" I asked.

"Not yet. But Azalea? I'm never going back out there. Willis is dangerous."

I turned Willis around in my head with that word, *dangerous.*

"Sorry I made you ride to his trailer. We never should have gone out there."

"You're right about that." Billy rolled his eyes and smiled

and I hoped we'd be friends again. We put the chicken in the kitchen icebox and headed back to the shade tree. We sat quietly, together. Billy wasn't laughing and telling me about his new school like always, but he wasn't leaving either.

Then, almost as if he'd known we were talking about him, here came Willis and his little sister strolling up like they owned the alley. Truly, I'd rather dunk my head in a bowl of maple syrup and lie down on a fire-ant hill than talk to Willis right now.

He stepped inside the fence, opened a piece of bubble gum, and broke off a piece. When he put it in his sister's hand, he whispered, "Don't say nothing." But I heard him.

I made myself look right at Willis. "What are you doing here?"

"I'm supposed to be here. Helping."

Helping, my left foot. Probably looking for a place for an afternoon nap. Willis sat his sister in a shady corner with her bubble gum. Took one piece himself and blew the world's biggest bubble.

I walked toward the spigot to turn on the hose and get away from Willis.

"Hey, Azalea." Oh, brother. Melinda Bowman, peeking around the side fence, wearing new white tennis shoes and even whiter socks. She handed me a plate of cookies.

"Mama heard the news last night. She's the main telephone operator."

"Thank you. I guess word travels fast in Paris Junction," I said. "Especially if Mrs. Bowman hears it first," I added under my breath.

Billy was already picking dead leaves off dried bean vines, so I said, "Help me water the fig tree. And Willis, just because Grandma Clark isn't *in* her garden doesn't mean she's not watching." He looked toward my grandmother's kitchen window, then picked up a shovel and snarled.

Before long, it was so hot, prisspot Melinda was wiping sweat off her face with a lace hankie. She sat down and took off her tennis shoes. Admired her nail polish, then rolled her blue jeans up higher. Finally, she filled up a watering can and drenched the orange spider lilies and her red toenails. Willis stayed between his sister and Melinda, shielding Lizzie from that stuck-up girl. He shoveled a few dead stalks before he jerked his head in Billy's direction. "I'm not doing this. You've got *him* to help. Everybody knows Chinamen love to work."

The back of my neck prickled up with heat and exasperation and I clenched what was left of my nails into my palms so hard they stung. "Why do you have to be so hateful?"

Willis stuck his chin out, his face the exact color of Grandma Clark's ripest tomato. Now he stood so close that his words were like spit bouncing off Billy's forehead. "You think you're smarter than anybody. Faster, too. Coming to our school to show off."

"What are you talking about?" Billy said.

"You're gonna hate it. Don't belong here. Won't have friends. Too skinny and scared of your own shadow. All you can do is work at that dumb grocery store and run fast."

All *I* could do right now was remember how much I hated

1.  talking
2.  talking to boys like Willis
3.  being in charge of my grandmother's garden and these blasted helpers.

But Billy Wong was my friend.

"Why do you care if Billy runs fast?"

"None of your beeswax, Miss Goody Two-shoes. But everybody knows I was going to be the junior high track star. Till *he* came along."

"It's called a track *team*, Willis. For a reason," Billy said. Then he did what my daddy tells me is the best solution to hatefulness. "Tell Mrs. Clark I hope she feels better. I'll be back to help later." He stood up taller, turned the other cheek, and headed toward his bike.

Lizzie scooted up to her brother. Her lip quivered and snot was running out of her nose and I didn't even care. Willis was nothing but mean. Glancing toward the kitchen, I prayed my grandmother would perk up, march outside, and tell these helpers to go away. I wanted her standing by my side, blessing Willis out.

But there wasn't a sound coming from the house because Grandma Clark was still asleep. I took two very deep breaths to make my heart slow down. "Go home, Willis," I hollered. "Don't come back. I mean it!"

Willis grabbed his sister's hand and marched her toward the back alley. Before he left, he took out his big wad of chewed-up Bazooka and jammed it right on the side of the garden shed.

Wait till I tell Grandma Clark all the bad things that boy did. Being hateful to Billy. Not working in her garden like the judge said. Breaking into our shed. She and that Miss Partridge lady would haul Willis DeLoach off to jail and hide the key.

But I couldn't blab to my grandmother. She'd know I hadn't told her the truth last night.

After everybody cleared out and I put away the tools and garden hose, I needed peace and quiet. Before I made it to my room, I fixed a sandwich for Grandma Clark and poked my head in to see how she was feeling.

She was struggling to sit up in bed, asking a million questions. *Get me some iced tea with this sandwich, Azalea. Can you prop up my pillows better? Did those helpers trample all over my rosebushes? Did you ever figure out why my shed light was left on?*

I told her we'd watered her fig tree and the spider lilies. That Mrs. Wong had sent a chicken and Melinda made cookies. I did not tell her Willis was mean to Billy again or that Willis and his sister had trespassed. I especially didn't confess that my stomach was tied up in knots tighter than her tomato stalks.

By the afternoon, Grandma Clark had dozed off listening to her radio show. I carefully wrote a note in my best script and left it on the table next to her reading glasses.

*Gone to Lucky Foods.*
*Be back soon.*

       *Azalea*

# Chapter 18

The vacant lot across from the grocery was full of boys and baseballs. And a whole lot of whooping and hollering.

Guess who was standing next to the tallest boy, running around like crazy catching fly balls. My friend Billy, that's who. I watched from the other side of the street till Mrs. Wong motioned from the door.

"Thanks for letting me play!" Billy called out, and he disappeared inside. By the time I walked through the front door of Lucky Foods, he was behind the counter, reading the scraps of paper under the glass.

"Hey, Billy. What're you doing?" Even when I squinted hard, I couldn't make out the squiggly writing.

"Notes from my great-uncle." Stepping around the cash register, he tapped the counter with a pencil. "You here to shop?"

His huge smile and him not staying mad at me made me whisper a confession. "Escaping Grandma Clark. I'm fed up with her."

"Really?" Billy pushed the pencil behind his ear and looked me straight in the eye. "She counts on you now."

"I'm sick and tired of people counting on me. I'm ready to go home to Texas and stop worrying about her falling in the garden." I was also sick and tired of worrying about Willis and Lizzie in the shed. But nobody could know that. So I changed the subject.

"Saw you out there throwing balls with those boys."

"Since that lot's so close to Lucky Foods, I catch with them when it's slow in here. Great Aunt keeps an eye on me from her kitchen window." He nodded toward the closed door at the back of the store and lowered his voice to almost a whisper. "Sometimes I think my great-aunt has Superman's X-ray vision. She sees everything I do!"

Then he laughed and said, "But you can cheer me on any time. Or come play with us."

I remembered Daddy teaching me to catch a ball. It was a disaster.

"I'm better at watching. Far away from a baseball. From across the street, even." Billy talking about his great-aunt's superpower reminded me of what my grandmother had told me. "*Superman*'s showing at the movie theater outside of town. Grandma Clark promised she'll treat us when she's feeling good enough to drive. If that ever happens."

"Tell her no thanks. I can't leave the store that long."

Was Billy still mad? I didn't want him even a little bit mad. "Then you wanna ride bikes with me?"

Billy's head jerked straight up and his glasses slipped down on his nose. "Not to the DeLoaches' pecan grove."

"Nope. Not a chance."

"Then maybe. But right now? I need to collect my school supplies." Billy reached way under the counter. He held up a mimeographed list: *Paris Junction School System. Seventh grade, 1952–53.* "English, world history, PE." He started reciting his class schedule by heart. "I can't wait."

Oh, brother. I couldn't help it. I rolled my eyes. "You're excited about school. I'm hoping to get back to Texas before all the recess buddies have been decided and my best friend's been dibbed by somebody else."

"Maybe you're better than you think at making new friends."

"Not so sure about that."

"My sister, May Lin, says trust somebody first. Before you make them a friend for life. She's worried I want to be friends with everybody." Billy laughed again. His laugh always made me smile. "May Lin says they might not be the best kinds of friends."

"Your sister's right."

"Paris Junction School has a party before the first day. For everybody to meet us new students." Billy tucked his chin down. He didn't look at me like he usually does. He wasn't smiling now. "I don't think I'll go."

"I don't like parties either. I'm better one person at a time."

Now his voice was so soft, I had to lean in to hear. But the grocery store got quiet, too, like it was listening for something important. "My sister worries some white students may not want me at the party. Or their school. People like Willis, maybe."

"Where does Willis think you should go to school? He doesn't get to tell you what to do!"

"The reason I moved here to live with my great-aunt and uncle was to go to a school like Paris Junction. In Shallowater, Chinese students aren't allowed in schools for whites. The Negro schools I could go to had used textbooks and broken pencils." Billy's voice reminded me of my grandmother's the day she told me about how my granddaddy never got to know me. So very sad.

"Anyhow, Great Uncle's glad I'm here, glad I'm at a great school. But he can't let me off work for a party." His voice got stronger. "I hope he'll let me join the school newspaper."

When Billy grabbed a shopping basket, I followed him to the back corner. To the jars of bright yellow unsharpened pencils. Square erasers. Clean notebooks. He picked up a fat pen and a pot of black ink. He added a wooden ruler to his basket. "I'll buy the rest at Jay's Department Store in Shallowater," he said.

"If you stay here for school, won't you miss your family?"

"My parents come twice a week to bring things to Lucky Foods. Besides, this *is* my family. Great Aunt and Uncle. I even have cousins in Paris Junction."

119

I chewed on my lip, tossing around how a big family would feel. A sister and brother, aunts and uncles, cousins. Billy had them all.

Before I put a question together, the door banged open and a man stepped inside. Billy put down his school supplies and stood behind the counter. But I didn't want to talk to another complete stranger. Escaping to the back of the store, I counted pencils and notebooks till he slammed the door and left.

"Who's that?" I asked.

"He owned the other food store across Main Street. Fancy candy and fancier writing paper than Lucky Foods. Great Uncle says it closed last month. His business comes here now."

"He wasn't very friendly. Grandma Clark says everybody loves shopping at your store."

"Mrs. Clark even buys sewing patterns here. Gets advice from Great Aunt about making aprons. Maybe you'd like to learn?"

I held up my bandaged finger. "Almost cut this off with a knife slicing tomatoes. Sewing? With a sharp needle? Me?"

Before Billy could talk me into buying a Simplicity apron pattern, I said good-bye. Waving a stack of Big Chief notebooks, he held open the screen door. "See you around, Azalea!" he called.

I took a deep sunshiny breath outside Lucky Foods. The smell of new paper had reminded me of doodling pictures on the side of my arithmetic homework.

It also reminded me I'd be lucky to get back to Texas in time to buy *my* school supplies.

## Keeping Notes on Lucky Foods
## My Private File

The screen door pushes open.
The bell ting-a-lings.
A white man steps inside, tall, frowning.
Hat pulled close over his forehead.
Eyes darting fast
from Kay's Cookies to Dum Dum suckers,
cash register to cigar boxes.

"Need me some garden fertilizer," he snarls.
"Near the fishing lures," I answer, nicely.
He draws his words out.
"Bologna? Cheese? Bread?"
"Right this way, sir," I say.

I reach into the cool case of cheese and lunch meat.
Weigh a thick wedge of cheddar.
Punch the cash register's round buttons.

Hand the man groceries.
Watch him leave.

He'll go in my stories.
Mixed together with
track meets,
Future Farmers,
Student Council,
dusting soup cans,
pricing crushable cracker boxes.
And new friends.

*Property of Billy Wong, Spy*

# Chapter 19

I'd pedaled my bike almost to Ruby Street when I heard Billy's voice. "Wait up, Azalea! Great Uncle says if I'm not gone long, I can ride over to my new school. See the seventh-grade classrooms. Wanna come?"

Since Grandma Clark was surely sound asleep, I followed him. We propped our bikes next to bright yellow flowers planted around the Paris Junction School sign. "This place is gigantic! I'd get lost in a minute." But Billy walked right up to the front door. Even though anybody could see as plain as day it was locked tight, he rattled the handle. I reached out and put my hand on his. "It's locked. If you keep banging, we'll look like a couple of crooks!"

Billy jiggled the door again. "I want to see inside," he said.

When a man taller than even my daddy appeared not two feet away, I looked for a bush to jump behind. Pushing his sunglasses off his eyes, he touched the lanyard hanging around his neck. Criminy! Was he about to blow that shiny whistle?

I stepped around Billy, who isn't hardly as tall as me and just as skinny. So smushing up behind him wasn't making me disappear. I covered my ears, waiting for the blast that would bring Paris Junction's policemen running.

"You youngsters need something?" His voice wasn't as scary as he looked.

Billy answered, "I'm going to school here. Seventh grade."

The man leaned closer. "Are you the Wong boy?"

"I'm Billy Wong."

"I'm Coach Walker. Heard you're a runner, ready to break our track records. Once school starts, come by the gym. We'll get you fitted out in shoes and a uniform. Okay?"

Billy looked like he might sprint around the building right now! "Yes, sir," he said.

"Today the building's locked up tight 'cept for folks getting things ready." Coach Walker turned, then stopped and said, "Welcome to your school, Billy!"

My friend stared and smiled at that coach's back the entire way down the sidewalk.

"Wow. You're gonna be a track star. Like Willis said."

"Well, not exactly a star. At least not for a while." He stuffed his hands in his back jeans pockets and smiled some more. "My brother, Peter, was fast. But the Chinese Mission School where he and May Lin went didn't have a team. On the days Great Uncle could spare him at the store, the coach let him come here to run."

I remembered what Willis had said about running fast. "Is that the reason Willis is so mean to you? He's jealous?"

"Whether he likes it or not, it's my school, too." Billy pushed his bike toward a long row of windows, low enough to see through, then stopped. "Wonder which is my homeroom. I have the *best* teacher, Miss Jones."

"You do?"

"My sister's white friends from church told her about the teachers. Paris Junction's got clubs and sports and harder classes than the school I would have gone to back home." When he talked about his new school, Billy's eyes lit up as bright as Coach Walker's silver whistle.

126

"You're lucky to have a sister who tells you stuff like that."

Billy nodded, then pointed toward a window. "Hey, I think that's the cafeteria."

"Back in Texas last year, fifth grade, we packed lunches and ate in our classrooms. Or went home to eat." Remembering walking home, having Mama waiting with peanut butter and banana sandwiches? Made me wish I'd see her and Daddy soon.

Billy rubbed a summer's worth of dirt off a window-pane, then jumped back. "Hey, who's that?"

I cupped my hands around my eyes. "Willis? Willis DeLoach? What's he doing?"

Billy pressed his nose harder to the window. "Can't really see."

"Holy crow! Is he cleaning tables? Didn't think Willis did a lick of work unless somebody was holding a shovel over him." Willis's chin was almost dragging on the ground. "He looks like he'd rather have his fingernails pulled out one by one."

After a minute, Willis disappeared, then there he was again, with a bucket and a rag, scowling even more. I couldn't help it. When he got to the long table in front of us, I tapped the window and waved. Willis turned his back quick and hustled toward the boxes labeled *Mister Bee Potato Chips.*

Truthfully, my stomach twisted up thinking about Willis. He'd promised to clear out of my grandmother's shed. But if he's here working all day? Tonight, Willis will be back sleeping where it's safe.

Maybe I should spill the beans to Billy about him and Lizzie.

Before I could find the right words, Billy said, "That lady is his daddy's sister. She comes into our grocery store. Great Aunt told me she runs the cafeteria."

"Willis doesn't act like such a big shot wearing a white hairnet." The minute I said that, almost like he'd heard, Willis ripped off the hairnet. He slammed his palm against the window and leaned in so close I could just about see his freckles popping out.

Billy crossed his arms, staring back. "He can't hurt us. He's stuck inside. Can't say one mean thing about this being *his* school."

I flipped my head around to get my ponytails off my hot neck and the picture of Willis out of my brain. "I should go. Grandma Clark might need me."

Billy turned, then stopped. "Almost forgot. My sister's senior piano recital is the Sunday before school starts. Maybe you'd like to come? Mrs. Clark, too. My whole family will be there."

A piano recital. With *lots* of new people. But now that I was friends with Billy, it might not feel like a room full of hard-to-talk-to strangers. We jumped on our bikes and he whistled a song, kicking his feet off the pedals, acting crazy.

"Hey, wait a minute. My daddy sings that to Mama, spinning around our kitchen after supper, pretending they're on some island."

"My father does, too. But he just sings, no dancing."

Billy broke out into the funniest version of "Some Enchanted Evening," and I joined in. "You may see a straaaannnngeeerrrr!" we warbled together.

Both of us pedaled off, singing about enchanted evenings and crowded rooms like we were famous opera stars. When we got to Lucky Foods, I stopped my bike next to the phone booth.

"Hey, Billy. I just remembered. When I first came to Paris Junction, I wanted to call Mama and beg her to come save me. Almost every day."

"See, it's not so bad here." Billy walked his bike behind Lucky Foods. I waved good-bye, trying to balance my bike with one hand.

All the way home to Ruby Street, the leaving Paris

Junction thought flew out of my head like blackbirds soaring out of our garden. I was singing, pedaling, smiling. So happy that for a minute I clean forgot about that sneaky skunk I'd practically invited to live in my grandmother's shed. Oh boy. Now what?

# Paris Junction School
# Observations

1. Sidewalks swept.
2. Flowers planted.
3. Cafeteria ready.
4. Coaches with sports equipment
   and practice times.
5. Clubs, school supplies, school calendar:
   lists all sent.
6. No broken chain-link fences.
7. No cigarette butts near back doors.
8. No bad words scribbled.
9. Big sign on marquee:
   WELCOME TO PARIS JUNCTION
   JUNIOR AND SENIOR HIGH SCHOOL!

*Billy Wong, New Student*

# Chapter 20

I walked into the house quietly, not like a herd of wild buffalo.

"Azalea?" My grandmother's voice drifted down the hall.

"Hey, Grandma Clark. Looks like you're feeling better." I fluffed her pillow and checked her water glass.

She struggled to sit up. "You missed Dr. Wiggins. He says I'll be right as rain in no time."

I didn't ask how much time was no time. She sure as shootin' needed me now.

By bedtime after I tucked her in and dragged myself upstairs, I was ready to collapse. But I kicked off my thin white sheet and flipped my pillow over a billion times. Too worried to sleep and too hot to breathe, I opened the window next to my bed.

Was that a light shining inside the shed?

I knew they'd be back! My heart raced with worry. What if Willis was messing around in Grandma Clark's things? Breaking cups and saucers. Getting into her collection of feathers and paints and canvases. He was mad as everything when we caught him wearing a hairnet and white apron. And washing their clothes at their trailer. Maybe he was mad enough to do something awful!

I should march out there and order him to leave. But truthfully, I was still a little afraid of Willis. I flopped back on my bed, listening to my pounding heart. Almost as loud as my heart, a huge moth was now beating its wings against the screen. Bump, bump, swish. Bump, bump, swish—over and over again. I'd never get to sleep. The moon was so bright, maybe I'd tiptoe outside, see what Willis was up to.

Hurrying down the back steps, then along the path, I squeezed both arms to keep from shivering. The shed was dark and quiet, the light now off. Where *was* Willis? My eyes shot up. Way up. And there he was in the moonlight.

"Willis! Why are you sitting on that branch?" I hissed.

He didn't answer.

"That you up there in the oak tree?"

"Keep quiet. You'll wake up Lizzie," he said, swinging down from a thick, fat limb to stand on the walkway.

I put my hand on my hip to show him I meant business. "You need to leave. When's your mama coming home, anyhow?"

He moved nearer the shed's door as if he could guard his sister. "Would have gone back to the trailer tonight. But Lizzie started crying."

Under the moonlight, I saw Willis had stuck out his chin and turned his cold shoulder my way. He'd acted terrible to Billy. Saying hateful things about going to his school. Even if I was worried about his little sister being scared, I'd never ever feel sorry for Willis DeLoach again. Once Grandma Clark's arm healed, I'd be back in Tyler, Texas. But honestly, I didn't want to leave her mad at me over somebody trespassing in her garden shed. Willis needed to go home!

"You'd better not tell anybody where you've been sleeping. Or mess up stuff."

Willis didn't say he'd keep quiet. Didn't even say thanks for letting him stay. He turned and disappeared into the shed, and I tiptoed back inside, shivering in the night air.

First thing I did was pull down my bedroom window shade, closing the moonlight away. I shut my eyes and pictured funny things to help me sleep. But honest to goodness, with Willis and Lizzie and my grandmother's garden shed jumbling up in my brain? It was hard to dream about somebody looking dopey in a hairnet.

# Chapter 21

Tossing and turning and looking at a loud ticking clock every five minutes does not make you fall asleep. Neither does counting hairnets or paper dolls or rotten tomatoes. But I'd *finally* shut my eyes when I heard a noise and looked at my clock again. Almost midnight! What was that noise? It sounded like a shower of little stones hitting the house. Peeking under the window shade, I saw somebody pick up another handful of whatever he was tossing.

Holy moly. Why was Billy Wong throwing gravel at my window? Was he waking up my grandma? Dr. Wiggins's medicine made her extra tired. I hoped she hadn't heard!

I threw my raincoat over my pajamas and jammed my feet into my tennis shoes without even unlacing them. I raced outside and grabbed Billy's hand. "What are you doing?"

What he was doing was gulping air and trying to talk at the same time. "They took Great Uncle off in an ambulance."

"Oh no! What happened?"

Even though there was hardly a breeze fluttering in the night air, Billy's teeth were chattering. "He may have had a heart attack."

Tears sneaked down behind his glasses. I looked the other way. "A heart attack?"

"Somebody threw rotten eggs. At the store's sign. And a big rock. Broke the glass. Scared us all!"

"Who would do that?"

Billy shook his head, slowly catching his breath. The porch light hit his black hair, his glasses, his face. "The meanest boy in Paris Junction," he said. "My archenemy, Willis DeLoach."

"Willis? Why?"

"Getting back for not letting him in the store? For you and me snooping around his house? Seeing him acting helpful? Laughing at that hairnet? I don't know."

I chewed on a fingernail for the hundredth time since I'd come to Paris Junction. "I don't think it was Willis."

"It was Willis all right. He's sure I want to take his place on the track team. He's mad at my great-uncle for reporting he was shoplifting."

But it *wasn't* Willis. When the grocery store's window shattered, Willis and Lizzie were sound asleep in my grandma's garden. And if Grandma Clark finds out they're sleeping in her precious room—full of things she cares about—and I hadn't told her the truth, I will be in bigger trouble than Willis.

"My family warned me to stay away from him. If they hear I went to play with that dumb puppy? They'll be mad." Billy grabbed my arm. "I had to come tell you that, Azalea. Nobody can know we trespassed on their property."

"I won't say anything. Promise."

"I'd better go. Great Aunt will be worried." He shook his head like he was trying to get rid of an awful picture, then whirled around and walked toward Main Street.

Behind us, my grandmother's bedroom window was dark, the house still and quiet. The honeysuckle's sweetness filled the air and mixed with things I didn't recognize, smoke or firecrackers, or maybe pure meanness. I was shivering and my stomach was in knots. But Billy was my friend. He needed me.

"Wait! I'm coming."

Billy's bright white T-shirt lit up in the moonlight, but the sidewalk was dark and bumpy and I stumbled. Billy didn't even notice. By the time I was close enough to touch his arm, he'd scooted across Main Street.

An idling police car beamed light on broken glass, on the glistening yellow egg yolks dripping down the door. Red paint splattered the crooked Lucky Foods sign. Even though it was past midnight, people gathered on the sidewalk, shaking their heads and talking. Billy walked closer to the store and a Chinese lady hugged him. Behind them, a little girl sobbed her eyes out. He pulled away, asking, "Is Great Uncle going to be okay?" They disappeared behind the grocery before I heard the answer.

"See you later?" I called. But Billy had vanished into a circle of family. A policeman holding a small notebook walked toward me. Standing in my raincoat and pajamas, I froze.

"Aren't you a little young to be out here by yourself?" he asked.

My tongue was thick in my mouth and my heart pounded so hard I couldn't talk. When he reached down to pick up something shiny on the sidewalk, I dodged behind a car. I ran all the way to Grandma Clark's.

I hoped she was still sleeping. I wasn't ready to talk. What would I say about *anything* that happened tonight? I tiptoed by her closed door and up the stairs.

Outside my window, I heard that gigantic moth flapping against the screen again, and I put my hands over my ears, tight. I squeezed shut my eyes. But I couldn't escape the memory of Billy's tears. Or of people huddled together, pointing at the shattered window and the ruined Lucky Foods sign.

# Crime on Main Street
## The Reporter's Five *Ws*, Just the Facts

1. When?

   11:30 p.m., August 10, 1952.

2. Where?

   Lucky Foods.

3. What I heard:

   Bang! Glass breaking. Feet running.

   What I saw:

   Yellow egg yolk, sticky and runny.

   Smeared over the *Lucky* in the Lucky Foods sign.

   Red paint, ugly and bright. Not good-luck red.

   What I smelled:

   Rotten eggs and maybe firecrackers.

What I know:

My friend says everybody loves my family.

Somebody must not.

What I feel:

Sick to my stomach.

But newspaper reporters aren't supposed to
write what they feel.
Just the facts.

4. Who?

I don't know.

5. Why?

I don't know.

*Billy Wong,*
*Reporting from My Cot Next to the Kitchen Door,*
*Behind the Grocery Store*

# Crime on Main Street
## How I Really Feel

Torn up inside.
Like a jagged chunk of broken glass has sliced my
heart in two pieces.

One piece wants to knock Willis down.
Grind my shoe's heel into his thick head
until he says sorry.

The other punches
my pillow.
All
Night
Long.

*Billy Wong, Mad as Everything*

# Chapter 22

Early the next morning after I'd run away from that policeman at Lucky Foods, I tiptoed to our kitchen. Remembering the smell of those rotten eggs closed my throat up, but I grabbed a banana and a glass of water and stared out the back door. One thing was for sure: Billy and his family had each other. Willis was my problem. Scary or not, I knew what I needed to do.

After a quick glance back at my grandmother's bedroom window, I tapped on the shed door. Nobody answered. The key was under the roof eave. I opened the door and whispered across the morning light. "Willis? Lizzie?"

They were gone. Not even a muddy shoe print left behind. Grandma Clark's china collection was safe on the shelves. But a big chair was pulled out like somebody had slept there. I leaned over to push it under the desk, stumbled, banged my knee, and let out a loud "Ow!" When I grabbed my knee, my sandal hit a cardboard box. It spilled open. Letters fell out. All over the floor.

I picked one up. Then another. They were addressed to me! Grandma Clark's beautiful writing slanted across every single sealed-up envelope. The same script that was on my birthday card and on her note inviting—no, ordering—me to Paris Junction.

But on these letters in my mama's handwriting, *Return to Sender* was scribbled across the envelope. Why hadn't she read them to me?

Stuffing three letters in my pocket, I put the shoe box back under the desk.

Then I pulled it out again. I shouldn't take them. Somebody had carefully hidden the letters in the shed. I should put them back in the box, sealed up, as neat as I found them. Billy says it's against the law to mess with somebody else's mail.

But these were mine.

So I kept the letters, locked the shed door, hid the key, and tiptoed back inside.

While Grandma Clark was still sleeping, I took one out and smoothed the envelope flat on the table.

*Azalea Ann Morgan*
*321A Hillcrest Street*
*Horseshoe Bend, Texas*

Our apartment when I was in first grade.
The second letter was addressed

*Azalea Ann Morgan*
*RFD 3*
*Shamrock, Texas*

We had to ride a bus into town. Daddy claimed good luck grew on the trees at the little farmhouse we rented. Turns out, it didn't.

I flipped the envelopes over. On every back flap, the same address.

*Mrs. Robert C. Clark*
*14 Ruby Street*
*Paris Junction, Arkansas*

All those places Mama, Daddy, and me lived, the different houses and schools and streets? My grandmother has lived on Ruby Street in Paris Junction since forever.

Before I could unseal a single letter, I heard Grandma Clark's cane clacking! I stuffed them in my pocket just as she hobbled into the kitchen, one arm in a sling and her gray hair sticking out every which-a-way.

She propped her cane next to the sink, sank into a chair, and pursed up her lips like Mama does when she's mad. "Azalea? Do you have something to tell me?"

"No, ma'am." I didn't think Grandma Clark had X-ray vision. So she couldn't know I'd found her letters. I picked at a rough edge of my thumbnail. I didn't bite it this time. I was trying to keep a promise to Daddy about my fingernails.

"The telephone rang. Woke me up. Where were you?"

In her shed looking for Willis and his sister, snitching my letters. "Guess I was brushing my teeth and didn't hear," I fibbed.

"Melinda's mother called. Mavis Bowman, the operator."

Uh-oh. Could *she* see me all the way from the telephone company across town? Did she know I was outside opening the shed door? I took a sip of the water I'd left on the kitchen table and tried to act normal. I couldn't tell anybody about Willis and Lizzie in the shed. Anybody, right now, meant my grandmother, of course.

"Mrs. Bowman called to say Melinda had choir practice and couldn't help today."

I breathed easier. For about a second.

"Told her I didn't need help today. Of course, she had to gossip about a ruckus at Lucky Foods. She took the call for Dr. Wiggins." Grandma Clark leaned in close and held my hand tight. "I thought I heard something late last night. Or did I dream that siren racing toward downtown?"

I couldn't confess I'd sneaked off to Mr. Wong's store long after I was supposed to be asleep, so I answered, "Want me to go find out?"

Grandma Clark leaned back, twisting the unraveling edge of her scarf sling. "I should call the Wongs. But I hate to disturb them if things aren't right."

"I'll go. I ate breakfast already." I held up my banana peel.

"Jump on your bike. Go see what's what."

I already knew what was what. The Lucky Foods grocery store had been vandalized. The Wongs blamed Willis DeLoach. Willis and Lizzie had slept in my grandmother's off-limits shed.

And somebody—possibly me—was gonna be in big trouble.

As I pedaled toward Lucky Foods, two thoughts played in my head like a broken record. *Grandma Clark can't find out I knew Willis slept in her shed. Mr. Wong needs to be okay. Willis in the shed. Mr. Wong okay. Okay, okay, okay. Please.*

But things weren't okay. The minute I stopped my bike, I saw a lady scrubbing caked-on raw eggs from the Lucky Foods sign.

Inside, the sun streamed in and landed on the counter, making me think of my first time here. Back when I was afraid I'd never be able to talk to Billy or his great-uncle. The day Willis's pocket change rolled under the cash register and he hightailed it outside with Mr. Wong mad as the dickens.

I squeezed my hands together to keep from shaking, and I walked toward the bins of pears and apples. "Hey, Billy. How's Mr. Wong?" I asked.

Propping his broom against a shelf of detergent boxes, he said, "Can't talk about it now," and he disappeared behind a neat shelf of Martha White Flour bags.

The air inside Lucky Foods wasn't moving. I had to get out of here. To run as fast as I could back to Grandma Clark's. But Billy was my friend. Why didn't he want to talk?

I stepped away from the shelves and toward the broken glass. "Want some help? I could sweep up."

Billy kept his back to me while he straightened soup cans, but his voice was quiet and steady. "If Willis DeLoach did this, and it was because he was mad at me for trespassing on his property, I'm not sure you and I can be friends."

Tears rushed into my eyes before I could even answer. When you only have a few friends, you don't like it when they're mad. Or sad. I had to tell Billy the truth about Willis and Lizzie.

"It wasn't Willis," I said quietly. "I promise."

Billy turned around and took off his glasses, cleaning them on the tail of his shirt. "Don't make promises you can't keep, Azalea."

I stared at the broken glass, the toppled-over cereal boxes near the front window, the red paint. Anywhere but looking Billy in the eye. "Willis and Lizzie were sleeping in my grandmother's garden shed," I said. "All night."

Billy's mouth flew wide open. "What? Her shed?"

"They sneaked in because Lizzie was afraid to be by herself. I didn't know till I caught them out there."

"You should report it to the authorities. Or at least to Mrs. Clark."

I followed Billy to the door of Lucky Foods, brushing past the cooling box full of milk bottles. But it wasn't ice making me shiver. "I can't tell! My grandmother doesn't allow anybody inside that shed, and Willis and Lizzie *slept* there."

"My family told the police sergeant Willis did it. Sooner or later, the police are going to ask about him."

"Oh, brother. I hope it's later," I said. "Because first, I need to figure out how to tell Grandma Clark the truth."

# Chapter 23

Instead of rushing back to Ruby Street, I followed Billy outside. He walked fast, leading me somewhere, saving me from confessing to my grandmother. For now.

People came in and out of other stores, pulling away from the gas station, driving slowly by Lucky Foods. Some of them whispering, some gawking. If my mama hadn't liked how everybody in Paris Junction knows your business, she'd hate hearing the gossip now. Billy ignored it.

Until Melinda Bowman bopped out of Ward's Drugstore, smack-dab in front of us. She's pretty hard to ignore, flouncing her curls and smiling her gigantic fake smile.

"Hey, Billy. I hear your great-uncle had a heart attack. Hope he's okay."

"He's going to be fine" was all Billy said.

"I betcha Willis made that mess of your store. Word is, the police are after him."

Now how in the Sam Hill did Melinda come up with that? Two nickels says her mother listened in on the police call.

"We don't know what they think," Billy answered, more polite than he needed to be.

"Just wait. It was Willis. You'll see." She beamed another fake smile, then crossed the street.

My heart was beating so fast, I couldn't talk. That's all I needed. Melinda spreading rumors. The police after Willis. My grandmother hearing the stories. Me and my big fat fib in the middle. I'd better confess to Grandma Clark this very minute.

Before I could take off running, Billy stopped in front of the Paris Junction History Room. He held his head way up, his shoulders, too. "Something I want to show you," he said.

We stepped inside, and I took a deep breath of the room's dusty coolness. "What's all this stuff?"

"The town's history. The librarian next door doesn't mind if I come in anytime. Some days it's open. Sometimes I ask for the key."

Once my eyes adjusted to the dimness, I sank into a soft chair that smelled like a rainy day. I tugged the desk lamp's chain to shine light on a book of old pictures. After a while, even though I heard the outside noises—cars slowing down, people talking—if I shut my eyes, the bad memories vanished into the room's quietness. I understood why Billy wanted me to see this special place.

"When the grocery's not too busy, I sneak over here. Where nobody will find me. But Azalea? Don't tell anybody." Billy laughed. "It makes me sound like I don't like having friends. You know, hanging around here by myself?"

I opened my eyes, blinked away the shadows, and laughed louder than Billy. "You? Not wanting friends? You even wanted me for a friend."

Now Billy had scooted in front of a big photograph hanging on the wall. A tiny sunlight sliver beamed in from the window. I slipped my bare feet back into my sandals to walk across the dusty floor. "What's this picture?"

He took his handkerchief out of his pocket and wiped the glass. "This is what I wanted to show you. Great Uncle donated this photograph. See that?" One thumbtack on the curled-up label had disappeared. Billy straightened it and read out loud. *"William Wong and Billy Jue Moon. Building the railroad from California, 1867. Our family moved to Arkansas and Mississippi right after the railroad was finished. We've lived here a long time."*

"Grandma Clark says everybody loves the Wongs."

"Guess not *everybody*," he said.

"Do you think they'll figure out the real culprit who messed up your store?"

"Whoever vandalized Lucky Foods didn't care who they hurt. Great Uncle hopes the police will handle it properly."

"I hope the police don't *handle it* all the way to believing Willis is guilty."

We stood side by side next to the picture, being quiet together. I could escape to this room all day. But I needed to get back. Grandma Clark would worry. Finally, we walked down the hall to open the front door.

And I almost slammed it shut!

Because there on the sidewalk was none other than Willis DeLoach, clutching a bottle of Coca-Cola. When he noticed Billy behind me, he banged his hand hard onto the door frame. "You hiding in here? What's going on? Cops asking everybody questions."

I don't know if I'll ever get used to talking back to a boy

as mean as Willis. But I took a deep breath and spit out, "Somebody threw rotten eggs at Mr. Wong's grocery store. What do you think about that?"

"Don't look at me. I don't know nothing." Willis could glare all right, but that's all he *said* before he pushed his way in like he owned the History Room.

I looked behind Willis. "Where's your sister?"

"None of your business, but she's with our aunt at the cafeteria," he muttered.

I worked to bring up a picture of Willis in a hairnet or Lizzie and her puppy. To keep me from being so mad. But all I saw was Willis flipping through the pages of a yellowed newspaper like it was the funny papers, instead of something old and valuable.

"Be careful with this stuff, Willis. You might learn a thing or two. Billy just moved to Paris Junction and he knows more about your town than you do."

Willis puffed up his chest in Billy's direction. "A squirt like you *would* hang out with this creepy junk. Not me. My first-grade class might've come here. My friends and me got better things to do now." He picked up a wooden box filled with arrowheads and shook it hard.

Billy put his hand on the box. "You're not supposed to mess things up."

Willis snarled, took a swig of his Coke. "I don't need you telling me what to do." His eyes settled on the big photograph of the men standing in front of the locomotive. "What's that?"

"A long time ago, Billy's relatives helped build train tracks across the country all the way from California." I looked again at the Chinese men pushing wheelbarrows, loading rocks.

Willis elbowed me out of the way. He smacked the wall next to the photograph. "Nothing but a bunch of stupid coolies."

In my whole entire life, I'd never heard that word. But the way Willis DeLoach spit it out, I knew calling Billy's ancestor a coolie wasn't something nice.

Billy's hands turned into two hard fists. "Watch what you're saying."

Willis spun around and stomped out. Outside the History Room, a bottle smashed loud against the brick wall. My heart jumped into my throat.

Billy stood in the dim room, shaking his head. "I'm leaving. I need to see about the store."

*I* needed to chase Willis down, grab a big sliver of glass off the sidewalk, and stab his eyeball out. But he disappeared into the bright sunshine and all I could think about was getting him out of our garden. Quick.

# To Azalea: What I Didn't Say

1. *About*
   notes under the glass on the store's counter.

   They may look like chicken scratch.
   To me, the Chinese writing tells
   what time the milk delivery arrives.
   Who owes Great Uncle money.
   Groceries ready for delivery.

2. *About*
   *Superman* movie.

   Great Uncle always needs me to work.
   It's my responsibility.
   I've never been to a picture show.
   My sister, May Lin, says
   I wouldn't even know where to sit.

3. *About*

   the History Room.


   Keep Willis away.


4. *About*

   shoppers at Lucky Foods.


   Some come in, go out. Hardly talk.

   Think we don't speak their language.

   Think if they ask hard questions

   about something besides fishing lures,

   sewing needles,

   sacks of flour,

   we would never understand.

   Never answer.


   Great Uncle, Great Aunt, and I

   can't believe they don't add grocery prices

   in their heads!

   Choose the freshest carrots.

   Grow spinach from packets of seeds.

We never laugh at shoppers like Mrs. Clark.

But when others open the door to Lucky Foods,

we whisper quiet words in our own language.

And behind our hands, we smile.


Your Friend, Billy

# Chapter 24

When I opened the kitchen door, Grandma Clark peered over her coffee cup and raised her eyebrows in a big question. "Well? What did you find out? How are the Wongs?"

"Somebody tossed raw, smelly eggs at their store. Mr. Wong almost had a heart attack. But I think he's okay."

"My goodness!" Grandma Clark slammed down her cup. "Who would do that?"

"The police don't know yet. The Wongs think it was Willis DeLoach."

But I knew. No matter how mean he is, no matter how much he doesn't like Billy or how mad he was at Mr.

Wong, Willis wasn't about to leave his sister sleeping in a dark shed.

My grandmother hobbled to the sink and dropped off her coffee cup. "That boy needs a strong hand to keep him out of trouble. What a disaster."

"Billy's whole family is cleaning up the store and visiting the hospital." I'd save the rest of the story till I'd figured out how to confess.

Grandma Clark chewed on her bottom lip, exactly what I do when I'm worrying. "Glad Mrs. Wong has her family. Nice as it is when friends bring casseroles, it's special when your real family comes to help."

She was almost saying thank you to me.

"We'll send vegetables. For when they reopen the store." Grandma Clark untied her apron and folded it on the back of a kitchen chair. "I'm feeling sprightlier this morning. Let's get ready for the garden helpers."

Jiminy Cricket. It's always that garden and those helpers.

She walked around pointing to her ink pen, wooden Popsicle sticks, her scissors. Telling me to hand her this and hand her that. "Row markers, dear. We'll need to prepare our garden for fall."

Our garden. Fall. I eyed her black phone and wondered for the zillionth time if I'd truly get back to Texas for the first day of school. Or whether Barbara Jean had found a new friend as easy to talk to as Billy Wong.

"Azalea! Garden markers, please." Grandma Clark's sharp voice made me jump, but when I handed her the wooden sticks, she smiled. Maybe her project would keep her from asking more about Willis or Lucky Foods right now.

She picked up her fancy pen and drew tiny spinach leaves, chard with bright red stems, and brussels sprouts. The words were curly and beautiful, too, like mine when I won the handwriting contest. I held up Swiss chard. "You're better than my mama, who can't draw a stick man to save her life."

I think she blushed. It was hard to tell behind her glasses, with her gray hair flopped out of its bun and onto her cheeks. "Happy it was my left arm I fell on," she said.

Closing my hands in my lap, I felt the thin envelopes still stuffed in my pocket. If I asked her why a box of letters—written to me—was hidden in the garden shed, she might haul off and shake them loose, telling me to mind my own business. Or holler at me for sneaking into her shed. But the words spilled out. I couldn't grab them back.

"Grandma Clark, you know how you're always telling me to be truthful? Well, here's the truth. I went inside your garden shed."

Her smile disappeared. "You shouldn't have done that. There's nothing there of your concern."

"I'm sorry. I was curious. Sometimes Daddy says too curious for my own good. I might not like meeting a bunch of strangers, but I like finding out about them." I took another brave breath. "I found something that *might* be my concern."

Grandma Clark peered down her nose and fiddled with the garden markers. "Yours? What could possibly be yours in my garden shed?"

I pulled the letters out. My voice and my hand were shaking. "There's a whole box of them. Addressed to me."

She reached for one envelope, turning it over and touching my name. "Such a long while ago. Your granddaddy tried to hide them from me when they kept coming back. But I knew." Her voice got softer. "He saved them, every one. He missed JoBelle something terrible. He would have loved you, Azalea."

I stood up quick so she wouldn't see my prickly tears. With my back to the table, I rinsed the coffeepot, her cup, my glass, letting the hot water hit my fingers. I grabbed the side of the sink and held on, trying not to cry about never knowing my own granddaddy.

"But somebody sent the letters back? Somebody didn't want them?"

"Your daddy had the wanderlust. No way to raise a baby, all that moving around. I wanted you to move here, instead of all over kingdom come. But JoBelle didn't want my influence."

"She sure was glad to be influenced when you needed a helper to push your wheelchair. Water the garden. Wash dishes," I mumbled. When I turned, a wisp of a smile had started on my grandmother's face. I stood up straighter and smiled right back. "So she and Daddy could go gallivanting off to the Grand Canyon."

"I was about to tell you your mama called while you were at the Wongs'. To check on us. Your parents didn't go anywhere without you, honey. Just sent you a gift to let you know they missed you."

"Will they be here before my school starts?"

"I'm sure they will. I know you'd like to go home," she said.

"Yes, ma'am. But not as much as I did when I first got here." I sat close to her at the kitchen table and flipped the spinach marker back and forth between my fingers. I grabbed her hand, and the softness reminded me of that first day, when Mama squished our fingers together, all three of us. "Grandma Clark? Those cups and saucers and china plates in your shed? You paint them all?"

"A friend and I made little puzzles out of the images. Secrets we shared. Haven't painted in years. Hardly go in that shed these days. Your granddaddy thought my art was foolish. JoBelle wasn't interested."

"They're beautiful," I said.

Grandma Clark reached for the hankie tucked in her sleeve and blotted a corner of her eye. Then she laughed out loud. "When your mother was a child, that garden shed was my quiet place. JoBelle didn't sit still long enough to read a book, much less pick up a paintbrush."

"Mama's still like that."

"That child was more than a notion! When she got older, if the phone rang, I never knew whether it would be the operator gossiping or a neighbor telling me she and your daddy'd run my car into a ditch." Grandma Clark shook her head at that memory. "Always hoped for a daughter who'd share my interest in painting. Wasn't JoBelle."

I touched a broken fingernail, still trying not to bite it off. "Nobody knows this but my friend in Texas. I like to draw. I'm pretty good. Even tried to draw some of your roses."

Grandma Clark beamed. "You'll have to show me."

"I'm different from Mama like that."

"Everyone in a family is different, Azalea. And every family is different."

I pictured her staircase wall of photographs, sad-looking people connected to each other from way back. If you unraveled a ball of string from one picture to the next, would they all connect back to me? Maybe those frowns just meant they didn't like sitting in front of a stranger getting their picture taken.

"Those pictures lined up on the stairs? Any artists like us?"

"Heavens to Betsy, no! Those are mostly Mr. Clark's people. Not an artistic bone in their bodies." Grandma Clark winked. "Let's get this cleaned up." She lined up her garden markers and handed me a stack to put away. "You're a good friend, Azalea. You've been kind to Billy."

"Remember when I thought I wouldn't be able to talk to him because he was a boy? And Chinese?"

"Be careful about jumping to conclusions. Even about boys like Willis DeLoach." When she said his name, my heart was the thing that jumped. Right into my throat, pounded so loud I worried she'd hear it. "Sometimes things are harder to figure out than they first appear," she said.

Since I'd been in Paris Junction, here's what *I'd* figured out.

1. Grandma Clark and I have art in common.
2. Even when he worried about his little sister, Willis DeLoach could be mean as a snake.
3. If you're sitting in Texas with your cat in your lap and the postman delivers a fancy note that you're sure will ruin your summer? Well, sometimes it doesn't.

# Chapter 25

A few days after the mess at Lucky Foods, Billy appeared at our door holding a brown paper bag. "Good morning, Mrs. Clark. Great Aunt sent these. Thought you might want to make pudding."

"Thank you, dear." She opened the bag and a smell of ripe bananas drifted out. "How's Mr. Wong?"

"Much better. We're opening the store today."

"Good news, Billy!" I said.

Grandma Clark reached in her apron and pulled out her best clippers. "Look in the garden for some vegetables. While you're there, cut my Lady Banks roses for Mrs. Wong." She opened and closed the clippers, making sure I knew the sharp side. "Where's my cane? I'll show you how."

"If you fall again, Dr. Wiggins will definitely hang you up for crow bait, just like you said. Billy and me know everything about your garden."

For another second, my grandmother clutched her rose clippers. She finally handed them over. I put them in my shorts pocket and patted it twice.

Before she settled in her chair and opened her dopey cooking magazine, Grandma Clark looked right at Billy and asked, "Do they know who vandalized your grocery?"

"The police are working on it."

"I'm sure they'll do a thorough investigation." She smiled. My heart missed ten beats. When she started to ask more questions, I pulled Billy out the kitchen door. He could have talked to her forever. Right now, I couldn't.

I hurried to the back fence and stopped in front of the shed. "Mr. Jackson sanded and scraped and painted two coats on the door to surprise my grandmother. Just yesterday. Paint's not even dry."

"Nice." He touched the paint and pulled back a finger with a blue smear on it. We stood there admiring the door sparkling in the bright sunshine, being quiet one minute, talking about almost everything the next.

"Said he'd come back after school starts. I might not be here to see it finished."

Billy's head tilted to one side, then the other. "Hey, Azalea. If you had a superpower, what would it be?" His smile told me he already had his picked out.

"You mean like those *Superman* funny books you like?"

"Exactly."

"The power to be invisible? See how long it takes Melinda to put her hair up in pin curls at night. Hear what my mama and daddy say about Paris Junction, why they left."

"'Cause everybody knew their business?" Billy laughed, mocking me but in a nice way. "I want my power to be X-ray vision, like the real Superman."

"Don't think I'd like seeing blood and guts and bones inside everybody," I said, laughing right back at him. We walked together toward the last of the bean vines and cucumbers. But before we snipped off one single cucumber or green bean.

Before I clipped one rose off the bush where two butterflies had landed.

Before Billy finished explaining to me about Superman's X-ray vision.

We were interrupted.

By the meanest boy in Paris Junction, Arkansas.

Willis Big Roach, hollering from the tall oak tree.

An acorn came pelting down, one of the tiny green ones that hurt like the dickens. Or, according to my third-grade teacher, Miss Wood, could put your eye out.

"Willis? What are you doing up there?"

He broke off a hard branch, tossed it at a paint can. "Get away from here!"

When he chucked a stick and it hit me smack-dab on my bare arm, I yelled back at him. "Stop throwing stuff! You're gonna mess up the new paint!"

Willis launched a leafy branch that bounced off Billy's knee.

Billy headed straight for the back gate. He turned and said, "I'm leaving, Azalea. Great Uncle told me to walk away from Willis." He disappeared down the alley without a single vegetable or even a rose.

"Now look what you've done. Billy was supposed to get vegetables and you ran him off."

"What do I care. I've been climbing up here since way before *he* came to Paris Junction."

The last time I climbed a tree, back in Texas, I ended up with two skinned knees, a twisted ankle, and a vow not to do it again. And I'd never ever climbed a tree with somebody mean in it. But I needed to talk to Willis up close. I took three deep breaths and pretended I didn't mind boys like Willis. I even pretended he was nice.

Trying to avoid the thick thorns from the trellis roses, I pulled myself to a branch just below Willis. He kicked the air near me, sneered, and reached up under his T-shirt for something. Two somethings. Rolls of toilet paper.

Okay, he was not nice. I stopped pretending. "What are you doing?"

"Nothing." He stuffed one roll between a fork in the tree. He opened the other and tossed it up, caught it, then tossed it again. He nodded toward the new paint. "Wonder how close I can get."

I tried to snatch the toilet paper out of Willis's hands. But truly, I didn't want to let go of my branch. "You doing this because you're mad at me? What'd I do?"

"This was my tree till that Chinese boy came. Now every time I need to climb it, he's around."

When a breeze rustled the tree's leaves, I grabbed hold of a thicker branch and held on. "Ever think about being friends with Billy?" I asked, still not quite believing I was perched in a tree with Willis DeLoach. "Y'all *will* be going to the same school next year. May be on the track team together."

"So what, chicken squat. Billy Wong and me ain't nothing alike. Why does your grandmother even let you be friends with him?" He lobbed the toilet paper toward a can. Which was not quite closed and half full of blue paint. He barely missed.

"My grandmother *wanted* me and Billy to be friends. She says it's good to have friends who aren't exactly like you."

"Not to me, it ain't," he muttered. "Anyhow, what were you doing at my school? Spying? He better not blab all over seventh grade about me having to help in the cafeteria. And for sure you'd better not come to my pecan grove again."

"Billy doesn't care about seeing you cleaning cafeteria tables. Or hanging out your wash. Heck, he works in his family's store most every day."

Willis muttered between clenched teeth but I heard him, loud and clear. "I bet he doesn't have to wear an ugly hairnet and big apron."

"You did look pretty funny wearing that white hairnet." I shifted my weight closer to the trunk, farther from Willis, in case he hauled off and popped me.

"Shut up, Azalea. And get your ugly face out of my tree."

"It's not your tree. And it's not nice to say shut up."

I bit my lip hard. I'd never cried in front of a boy and I didn't plan to start today. And unless you count Freddie Davis in first grade who cried when he wet his pants and everybody scooted away from him at story time, I'd never heard a boy cry out loud. So when a few tears slipped out of Willis's eyes and he quickly turned his head, I changed the subject.

"You can see forever," I said. And it was true. The sky stretched clear to Main Street. "Is that why you like it up here?"

Willis scratched at a nasty brown scab that had started to bleed down his leg. You'd think once blood was running down your leg, you'd move on to doing something else with your hands. But not Willis. He kept picking like he was digging for treasure.

"I like climbing this tree 'cause I'm higher than anybody. And nobody bothers me." He blotted his knee with the bottom of his shirt. Oh boy, his mama's gonna tan his hide when she sees the blood on that shirt.

I moved a *little* closer, thinking maybe I could get that last toilet paper roll before he knocked the petals off a prize rosebush or toppled over a paint can. Trying to distract him, I said, "I'm going back to Texas soon."

"Thought you'd stay here forever."

Much as I still don't like talking to people I hardly know, especially people I don't like. Much as I'd rather be *under* a tree all by myself. Willis in a tree branch seemed easier to talk to. But he was still clutching the toilet paper.

"I hope my grandma doesn't find out you stole something valuable from her shed."

"I didn't steal anything!"

"That's what you say. Anyhow, I could get in trouble for not telling her the truth about y'all sleeping there." I looked down at the Timex watch Daddy gave me for reading the most books in third grade. "Where is your sister? Is your mama home yet?"

"Our cousins said me and Lizzie could stay with them till Mama gets well. We moved yesterday."

"Good. And Willis? The police are asking about what happened at the Wongs' store. They say anything to you?"

"Nope. We were here that night. For all I know, you messed up that grocery store." His voice was back to hard as nails. Daring me to tell my grandmother they were sleeping next to her art things.

I was more than ready to get out of this tree.

But first, I glanced up. In time to see Willis pick up that roll of toilet paper, haul off and aim it straight at the blue paint. He swung off one branch, then another, not even looking down. He jumped on his bike. Took off down the alley, fast. "Don't follow me, Azalea," he hollered back.

Next to the shed door, blue paint seeped onto the walkway like the sky was falling, piece by piece. I hurried to turn the big can right side up. At least there was one thing I could fix.

# Chapter 26

The next days were a blur of work and worry. First watering the garden, then running to Mr. Wong's grocery for milk. What's worse, every time I saw Billy, now that his great-uncle was feeling fine, all he talked about was *school this* and *school that*. All I could think about was me not telling the truth.

Then the doorbell rang.

It wasn't time for the garden helpers. My grandmother's neighbors walked right in with their casseroles and cakes. So who was ringing our doorbell? I clomped down the stairs in my cowboy boots and peeked through the front window.

Oh no! I should sneak out the kitchen door and take off!

The doorbell rang again, a long, loud buzz.

"Get that, Azalea!" my grandmother called from her room. "What's the matter with you, girl?"

"Nothing." I choked the word out so quiet I'm sure she didn't hear it.

Now the knocks were even louder than the doorbell. I inched backward, holding my hands over my ears.

Grandma Clark's cane clacked across the hall. "For heaven's sake, I'll get it."

When she opened the door, a tall policeman stepped inside. He took off his blue hat. Even from my hiding place squeezed beside the dining room cupboard, I knew. He was the policeman I saw at Lucky Foods!

"Afternoon, ma'am. This is a courtesy call about the vandalism over on Main Street. Just to let you know the DeLoach boy has not been charged. Probably won't be. Social worker lady says you're listed in his file as looking out after him."

"Willis has been helping me and my granddaughter in my garden. That's all." Grandma Clark held up her cane in case the policeman wondered why.

He shifted his hat from one hand to the other. "We're double-checking his alibi." He looked past her at me slinking away. "That your granddaughter? She a friend of his?"

Grandma Clark quickly turned toward the dining room. "Azalea, come in here," she said, her voice sharp as a crow's caw. I shut my eyes and counted to ten before I could face my grandmother and that policeman.

Pulling out a little notebook, he flipped through the pages. He looked up and smiled while I chewed my lip and fidgeted to keep my fingernails out of my mouth. "I'm Sergeant Steele. Willis DeLoach says he was with you when the Wongs' store was vandalized. Late at night, around eleven thirty?"

Grandma Clark took in a sharp breath and narrowed her eyes, waiting for my answer. But I couldn't get my voice to work. My grandmother would find out I'd been lying. Or they'd take me in for questioning. I didn't know which was worse. Me disappointing her or me being hauled away in the backseat of Sergeant Steele's police car.

"The good news is we found the culprit who damaged the store. Another businessman. Blamed the Wongs for his own store closing across the street."

My grandmother was shaking her head, the policeman was frowning, and all I could think of was racing out the door, running all the way to Tyler, Texas, and never coming back.

Grandma Clark jolted me out of that thought. "Azalea, speak up. You won't get in trouble if you tell the truth."

I'm not so great at being bad. So I confessed about Willis being in the shed because Lizzie was scared. That his mama was sick and they had a puppy.

I left out the part about him bribing Lizzie with stolen gum. Every other part was the truth.


When the policeman left, my grandmother sat on the sofa, her back straight as a garden hoe, and patted the cushion next to her. Her voice was softer now, but she meant business. "Sit here. Tell me exactly what happened."

"I'm really, really sorry, Grandma Clark."

"Only thing to be sorry about? Not telling me. You did what you thought was right. If I'd been myself, I would have taken them in. Or at least let somebody know they were in their pecan grove all alone."

"I don't even like Willis. He's been nothing but ugly to Billy. And he almost got me in trouble with you."

"You never know what folks are going through, Azalea. Most people don't want to let on when they need help. Like

Willis and little Lizzie out there alone. Maybe that boy was trying to do something right for once."

"Doesn't matter. He had no right to be mean to Billy."

We sat side by side for a long time, not talking. I don't think it was because she was mad. Really and truly, we both liked the quietness in the living room.

# Chapter 27

Before we'd finished breakfast the next morning, the hall telephone ding-a-linged. I counted the rings— long-long-short—before answering.

"Mama!" I hadn't heard her voice since she dropped me off in Paris Junction. Daddy had been the one calling, telling me he missed me, explaining they'd bought that paperweight at a store nowhere near the Grand Canyon. Mama had sent a postcard. She'd called Grandma Clark to check on her. But now, finally, I could tell her I wasn't mad she'd left me in Paris Junction.

Her voice sparkled through the party-line phone.

"We're coming to get you in time for school. Can't wait to see you, baby."

And guess what my first thought was? Not about Barbara Jean being my recess buddy. Not about buying new pencils and notebooks. Not even about how much I missed them.

The first words out of my mouth were "I can't leave before Sunday. We're going to my friend's sister's piano recital."

"We won't make you miss that. I promise," Mama said. But truthfully? Her sad voice sounded more than ready for me to come home.

Across the kitchen table, my grandmother sat quietly with her sewing basket, mending a bright yellow apron and smiling to beat the band.

A few weeks ago when she sent her message asking for my help, I hardly knew what to call Grandma Clark. The last thing I wanted to do was spend the end of my summer in Arkansas with a bunch of strangers. Now I hated to leave.

Two days later, Grandma Clark sent me to the shed.

I almost fainted off my chair. "The shed? Your painted china is there, all your brushes, your easel, those little canvases. What if I break something?"

We'd been lining up Popsicle stick markers. Sorting seed packets for her fall garden. But she held up a basket and shooed me out the back door. "I'll clear off the table. You go put the art supplies in this basket. We're making May Lin a gift."

The shed's blue door was still sticky from Mr. Jackson's hard work, but Willis hadn't messed up the paint too much. Inside, half buried under a pillow, a paper doll leg I hadn't noticed, wearing a red shoe, made me smile. The only sign that Willis and Lizzie had been here. I glanced at the box of my letters. Grandma Clark had told me what they said, how all she wanted was to know me better. I didn't need those letters. I had my real grandmother now.

After I carefully packed paint, brushes, and the smallest blank canvases into Grandma Clark's basket, I held my breath all the way to the kitchen. Hoping I wouldn't drop Billy's sister's present before I created it.

My grandmother spread newspapers and hovered over my shoulder, helping me, teaching me about painting on a canvas. "Use the smallest brush for the flowers, Azalea. And the lighter green shades on the stems."

After we set the painting on the chest to dry, I stepped back. The gift had a secret message, a lily of the valley. Because it's special for the month of May and her name's

May. And because the flower means happiness. "That was fun," I said. "We're good artists together, Grandma Clark."

She looked like she might float away on the clouds I'd painted. "Don't forget. Sign it there, on the bottom. Always sign your artwork, dear."

"Our names are almost the same. Alice Ann and Azalea Ann."

"I know that, Azalea. Always have." My grandmother lined the tubes of paint up in her basket, handed me brushes to clean, and I didn't even care that she forgot to say please.

# Chapter 28

O n the afternoon of the recital, I buttoned up the scratchy blue dress I hadn't worn since I left Texas, put on my Sunday school shoes, and wheeled Grandma Clark down the sidewalk. She was holding a tray of cookies. May Lin's gift was tucked into the side of her wheelchair. Her hat was pinned down just so and her dress was ironed so carefully you'd never know Dr. Wiggins had just taken a sling off one arm.

There was one thing we hadn't counted on. Ten steep steps, straight up to the big front door. That was ten more than Grandma Clark had tackled in a while.

"Goodness. I wasn't thinking. How am I supposed to get inside?"

"We can do it together. Leave the gift and the cookies. I'll come back for them."

Before I could take the tray, guess who came prancing down the steps of First Baptist. Melinda Bowman, holding on to another prissy girl.

She smiled her fakest of smiles at my grandmother. "Mrs. Clark, how are you feeling?"

"Better, thank you," my grandmother answered.

"Guess y'all heard they caught the person who damaged the Wongs' store," Melinda said. "That awful man who sold fancy food across the street from the gas station. I knew it wasn't Willis all along."

She knew no such thing. But I kept quiet. I'd made my friend this summer. His name was not Melinda.

"We had a special practice for the duet Sandra and I are singing next Sunday." She leaned close to the girl whose name must be Sandra, then spun around on her shiny shoes to face me. "Those cookies smell good. What are y'all doing here? Can I help?"

"We're invited to Billy's sister's recital. She has a music scholarship to college next year," I answered, looking at the cookies and my grandma. Not at Melinda.

Before Melinda could gossip about May Lin's piano playing or go on about how she could bop over and make cookies with my grandmother any old time, I pushed Grandma Clark closer to the steps. Truly, I didn't care to say another thing to those girls.

Thank goodness Billy rescued us. He was wearing a suit and a white shirt with a tie. "Hey, Azalea! You came!" he said.

Melinda and Sandra fluttered their fingers at my grandmother and skipped away. I hoped that was the last I'd see of Melinda Big Bow in my entire life.

Billy grinned like those stuck-up girls hadn't looked right through us both. "Leave the wheelchair under the tree. I'll help you, Mrs. Clark. My grandparents are already here. My parents couldn't come, though. Somebody had to run the grocery in Shallowater. They can hear my sister play any old time." He sounded disappointed, but he still waved and smiled to the people parking their cars in front of the church.

When we walked into the big Fellowship Hall, it was all I could do not to gasp out loud. I was getting good at talking to one stranger at a time, maybe two, but here was a whole roomful. For somebody whose favorite thing was sitting under a shady tree with a sketchbook or talking quietly to Billy or Barbara Jean, I had to push myself into the room.

A sea of beautiful colors, of ladies in high heels and fancy clothes, filled the folding chairs lined up near the piano. A few older people stood near the refreshment table, talking together in Chinese. Mr. Wong waved from the front row, and I tried to smile back. But my head was swimming from the sweetness of more flowers than I'd seen all summer in Grandma Clark's garden. When a tiny lady with her hair done up so pretty, wearing the most beautiful dress in the room, walked up, my grandmother straightened her hat and folded her gloves on top of each other.

Billy touched the Chinese lady's shoulder and smiled. "Yang Yang, this is Mrs. Clark and Azalea."

I said hello and talked to a person I'd never met. I am getting braver.

"I know you're proud of May Lin, such an accomplished musician," my grandmother said. "I remember when Billy's sister and brother worked with me at the Chinese Mission School's garden a few years ago." She and Mrs. Wong talked about how nice the tomatoes had been this summer and how pretty the flowers were today till Billy took his grandmother's arm and slowly walked to the front row.

Before the music started, my grandmother whispered,

190

"I suspect many of these guests are cousins, aunts, uncles. Billy has quite a large family, doesn't he? Look at the children worrying over Mr. Wong."

"Your family's getting bigger by the day," I whispered back. "Especially if you include all those frowners in the photos." She and I laughed together, and Grandma Clark touched the pearl pin holding her straw hat down, then patted my hand. I didn't let go until May Lin's beautiful playing stopped. That's when my grandmother and I dropped hands to wave across the room to Billy.

Even if Grandma Clark claimed I was doomed to have my daddy's devilish blue eyes, I knew she loved me. And I loved her, too.

# Great Uncle's Advice to Nieces and Nephews, Tacked to Our Kitchen Wall

I will write this into my stories.

Lucky Five
Words to Live By

1. Be honest.
2. Be generous.
3. Be polite.
4. Study hard.
5. Honor your elders.

*Billy Wong, Son, Grandson, Great Nephew*

# Chapter 29

Until Mama and Daddy came to take me back to Tyler, Texas, I was still my grandmother's Number One Helper. Tidying up the big dining room table, I held up a wooden Popsicle stick labeled *Bok Choy.* "Did you spell something wrong, Grandma Clark?"

"Heavens to Betsy, girl. Haven't you learned a thing at Mr. Wong's store? Bok choy's a delicious vegetable. Grows nicely if we have a warm fall. With luck, I should have enough to share with the Wongs' customers before Thanksgiving."

I fiddled with her ink pen, rolling it between my fingers. "Billy says he'll help you when I leave. But he's joining every club in the universe. That's all he's talked about since his sister's recital."

Grandma Clark sorted another garden marker into the right stack. "I imagine the helpers will come one last time. After that, I can manage on my own. The hard work's finished." She stood up and looked out the window to a bed of tall flowers, bright orange in the sunshine. "Let's dig up some of my spider lilies. I'll bag some up for Johnny Morgan. Should grow in Texas without much attention."

I'd never liked those creepy spidery flowers, but if she wanted to pass along anything from her garden to my daddy, I wasn't saying a word.

"First I'd better return Mr. Jackson's bike. You think he'll find me another one next summer?"

Grandma Clark smiled bigger than the cat on her kitchen clock.

By the time I'd cleaned off my bike good enough for somebody else to appreciate it and ridden all the way out to Henry Jackson's place, I needed a cold drink. Thank goodness he had a block of ice cooling his sweet tea. We poured ourselves glasses and sat at his picnic table.

Mr. Jackson's dog put her little head between her paws and looked up. "Tiny's gonna miss you, Azalea. Mrs.

Clark'll be sad when you leave, too." When he scratched Tiny's ears, I swear that Chihuahua was smiling at me.

"Took my grandmother a while to get used to me."

Mr. Jackson took a big sip of tea and took his time answering. "That's her way. She'll be counting the days till next summer, I guarantee. She and your friend Billy."

"Did you hear they caught the guy who messed up the Wongs' store?"

"Sure did. Some folks just don't know how to behave, do they? But I hear you helped Willis out of trouble."

"Don't know about that. At least I finally told the truth." We let the silence settle on that thought.

"When is Mary Josephine getting here?" Mr. Jackson asked.

"Mama? The same evening Billy starts school. My school starts a few days later. I'll be back in Texas!" I set my tea down on the ice block to cool it off, then held my glass against my cheek. *Back in Texas* didn't sound like such an emergency now. "I better go. Grandma Clark's got some last chore dreamed up for me, no doubt."

"Speaking of that, tell Mrs. Clark I'll finish painting the shed soon as I catch up with my bike fixing."

"Guess what, Mr. Jackson. Willis is doing it! Grandma Clark cooked up a deal. He has to put another coat on and

195

finish the windows since she let them sleep out there. Well, not exactly *let*. But you know what I mean."

Thinking about all the ugly things he'd said to Billy? Willis was sure to get in more trouble. Just like Billy was sure to be the star of the track team and the president of the school before long.

Mr. Jackson grinned big as anything. "Well, I'll be. Didn't know the boy had it in him to paint that shed like Mrs. Clark wants it."

I took a last sip of sweet tea and fanned myself with my hand. "Willis'll make a mess of it," I said. "Or end up sitting in a tree all day."

Without a bike it took me longer to get back to Grandma Clark's. But truly, I didn't mind how everybody waved and told me to have a nice day. Guess I was getting used to Paris Junction. Maybe I was getting braver.

When I got to the front of Lucky Foods, Billy was outside clipping dead leaves off geraniums. He stuck his clippers into his apron pocket and handed me a green plant. "Here's something for your grandmother, Azalea. Scallions, from the Chinese school's garden. I'd bring it over myself but I've got stuff to do before school tomorrow. Don't think it's too heavy for you to carry."

"Thanks, Billy," I said, and I took the clay flowerpot.

"Mrs. Clark and my great-aunt started that garden a while ago. Now that the school's closed, Great Aunt's trying to save the plants. Says these are good pickled."

I didn't want to insult Mrs. Wong so I didn't tell him pickled scallion bulbs sounded awful. But my face might have given me away. I changed the subject back to what Billy loved talking about. "You excited about tomorrow?"

"Wait for me when school lets out and I'll tell you about it," he answered.

Even lugging a flowerpot, I skipped all the way to Ruby Street. I didn't spill a bit of dirt or break off a green scallion. Grandma Clark would still have plenty to pickle.

# Chapter 30

On the day school started in Paris Junction, I took out my sketchbook to draw one last flower picture or maybe copy the shed's blue paint color. And there it was. With all the other things crowding up my head, I'd forgotten the broken plate.

This morning Grandma Clark had made her own breakfast. Mine, too. Last night at supper, we'd sat at the kitchen table side by side listening to her radio station. Yesterday she'd let me use her best clippers again. Now roses were the first thing Mama and Daddy would smell when they opened the front door. But when my grandmother saw this broken plate, all the nice things we'd done together could fall to pieces.

I took three breaths to get my strength up for confessing. Then I walked downstairs to the kitchen. Grandma Clark folded her white dish towel over the sink and asked, "Did you finish packing your valise, Azalea?"

If I hadn't been so nervous I would have smiled to remember the first time I'd heard that funny word, *valise*. "Almost finished. But first, I have something to tell you." I handed her the broken plate. "I wish I could glue it back. But there are too many pieces. It was so beautiful. I'm really, really sorry."

"Good heavens. I've broken a few myself. Can't count how many your mother shattered. Don't worry one bit. I have enough to last a lifetime." She dropped every single piece right into the trash.

She slid two decorated cups and saucers across the table. "These are for you to take back to Texas. I painted them when JoBelle wasn't much older than you are now. Keep them to remember your old grandma."

"Grandma Clark! I'm not forgetting anything!"

"Pack them carefully. They're pretty fragile."

Touching the painted flowers on the perfect cups, I

turned the saucers upside down. Her initials were signed on the bottom, like she told me always to do. I hugged her, then carried them upstairs. I carefully wrapped them inside my new pedal pushers, already packed, ready for the Tyler Elementary Back-to-School Picnic.

# Notes for My First Day of School

What I'm Most Excited About

1. *Tiger Times.*

2. Running track.

3. Studying hard.

4. Making friends.


What May Lin Tells Me

1. She will pick out my first day clothes.

2. I should clip my fingernails.

3. Be sure I don't smell like fish.

4. Sit in the front row.

5. Stay friends with Chinese.

     They will always be your friends.

6. Smile.


What I'm Afraid of on My First Day,

But Won't Confess to May Lin

1. Missing the early bell because of

     spoiled milk that needs wiping up,

soup can explosion,

meat cooler leak,

smelly fish delivery,

other Lucky Foods emergencies.

2. Hearing Willis call me names.


What Great Uncle Says about That:

*Turn the other cheek.*


But if I turn the other cheek,

I may not turn around again.

I may not smile again, like May Lin says I should.

Is it possible that May Lin

knows more than Great Uncle

about not looking down,

about turning the other cheek.

And about smiling?


*Billy Wong, One of the First Chinese*

*at the Paris Junction School*

# Chapter 31

Walking from Ruby Street to the Paris Junction School should have been easy. Except today was the hottest day ever. And I was a little worried about who I'd have to talk to. Today, all I really cared about was saying good-bye to Billy.

I got there before the last bell rang and I waited on a shady bench, watching the front door. Of course, Melinda and Sandra and their stuck-up friends came out first, giggling to beat the band. I pulled my knees up to my chest and made myself into an invisible ball.

They saw me anyway.

"Hey, Azalea. You waiting for somebody?" Melinda flipped her hair bow like always and shifted her brand-new book satchel from one hip to the other.

"I'm waiting for Billy."

"You hear about Willis?" she asked.

I shook my head.

Her friend spoke up. "He was in a bad fight. First day of school."

"And guess what," Melinda chimed in.

I was kind of speechless, so it was hard to guess what.

"He got a bloody nose. Spent all afternoon at the nurse. His nose looked like an elephant sat on it."

The three of them broke into a fit of giggling and gasping for air.

Oh, brother. I'll never like talking to girls like Melinda and her friends. Even about a creep like Willis. Lucky for me, they spotted the football team running around in their uniforms and I went back to being about as interesting as pulling up weeds in our garden.

But when Billy stepped outside, grinning like he'd already won the student council election, I jumped up and waved real big. "Billy! Over here!" He carried a pile of new books tight under one arm, his track shoes slung over the other shoulder.

Pretty close behind him? Willis came strutting out, nose bandaged and shirttail untucked. He looked toward the little kids' school next door, where Lizzie waved from the swing set. Then he darted out the door like he didn't see me and Billy. Kind of like that time we saw him in the hairnet and he tried to pretend he was invisible.

I already knew enough about Willis DeLoach to last an entire lifetime. But I had a zillion questions for Billy. "How was it? Did you like the teachers? Did you join the Future Farmers and the newspaper already?"

"Hold on, Azalea. Can't do everything on my first day." He sat next to me on the bench, swinging his feet and kicking up dirt, laughing, too.

I laughed right back. "Well, *you* might could. Me? If I joined clubs, I'd never say a word. If I raced around a track, I'd fall flat on my face."

But truly, if I've learned a single thing this summer, it's that even if you mostly love drawing flowers in your sketchbook, you can be friends with the boy who's class president.

Billy opened his notebook and pulled out a list so new it smelled like the mimeograph machine. "Paris Junction Seventh Grade Weekly Schedule. Look at this. I bet my school in Shallowater wouldn't have had half these activities. At my brother and sister's Chinese school, there were no sports and not many clubs. Hope I can figure out how to do everything and still help Great Uncle at the grocery."

Thinking about Lucky Foods made me curious enough to ask, "Did you see Willis fight? Melinda told me he got in a fight."

"Heard he mouthed off to one of the tenth-grade boys. Who hauled off and slugged him good. Principal punished them both. I bet Willis will have to put on his hairnet and scrub more tables."

"Willis had better mind his own business." I drew circles on the bench with my finger, then looked Billy right in the eye. "I sure hope nothing like that happens on my first day of school."

"I don't think you have to worry, Azalea. You won't have anybody like him in sixth grade." Billy's smile was brighter than the sun!

After he pored over his activities list, he folded it inside one of his brand-new books. Opening his Big Chief notebook to a fresh page, he said, "Write your address here."

On the straight lines, I wrote in perfect Palmer penmanship:

*Azalea Morgan*

*221 North Alamo Avenue*

*Tyler, Texas*

"Promise you'll send me the articles you write for the newspaper."

Billy said yes. I knew he would.

"I better get to the store. Lots of business when school lets out. Great Uncle will need me."

"I'll walk downtown with you. My parents aren't coming till suppertime. We leave tomorrow at the crack of dawn. Before it gets too hot."

We walked real slow back to Lucky Foods, first peeking in the window of the History Room, then the library. The waitress at Ward's Drugstore was standing by the comic books, maybe even reading one herself. She didn't look up. I didn't care. Billy was the one making me laugh with his stories.

After he said good-bye and "See you next summer, Azalea!" he disappeared inside the grocery store.

I couldn't *wait* till next summer.

———

I ran all the way to Ruby Street. Where Grandma Clark was in the kitchen, standing over a big canning pot. She added a pinch of salt and two heaping spoons of sugar. The more she stirred, the better it smelled.

"How was Billy's first day? I hope the other children were kind to him."

"Grandma Clark! We're not children!" This time I laughed with her. "Billy loves school in Paris Junction. He said he'll see me next summer."

She put the top on her pot and reached her hand out to take mine. Grandma Clark hugged me and I hugged her right back.

When she finally let go, she said, "Your parents should be here before long, Azalea. They're spending the night, leaving first thing tomorrow."

All our family. In one place. Would those fireworks my daddy teased Mama about every time she talked to Grandma Clark explode? Or would they now be friends? Like me and Billy, and me and my grandmother?

"Grandma Clark, you think you and Mama will get along under the same roof? You're not gonna say mean things about Daddy? You're not still mad at them, are you?"

"Your parents left here as soon as they graduated from

Paris Junction High School. Hardly took time to say good-bye. JoBelle took her daddy's heart when she left."

"Well, like you said, it was a long time ago."

"I expect we will move past that. It's what families do. Things work out."

I took a deep breath of the sauce simmering on the stove. The whole house smelled like tomatoes and sunshine and roses! I couldn't wait to see Mama and Daddy. To show off the garden, tell them about Billy and Willis and even prisspot Melinda. And right that minute, I knew as well as I can tell a ripe tomato from a green one that Grandma Clark would be fine without me. Her foot was healed and so was her arm. Maybe even her heart.

"I'll wait outside for Mama and Daddy," I told her.

Opening the back door, I stepped into our garden.

The first thing I did was look way up to the top of the oak tree to be sure Willis wasn't there to torment me.

Then I grabbed a handful of skinny branches, put my foot on the trunk, and I hoisted myself up in that tree. And I didn't slip. Not even a little.

# Author's Note

One of the things I love most about writing is discovering and sharing both small details and big ideas that might surprise readers. Historical fiction can't be written without research, and that's what drew me deep into Billy Wong's story.

When I began writing this book, I learned about the remarkable archives at Delta State University's Mississippi Delta Chinese Heritage Museum. There, I pored over oral histories, photographs, and artifacts of actual Chinese American grocers.

Even though I'd regularly shopped with my mother and my grandmother at the Modern Store in downtown Cleveland, Mississippi, and at Lee's Grocery, a store I could walk to on a nice day, I had a lot to learn.

In the Bolivar County Library System, I read that from the 1940s until the late 1960s, there were as many as 250 Chinese grocery stores in the region, just like Lucky Foods. There were close to 50 in Greenville, one of the larger towns in the Mississippi Delta. My own hometown's 1955 city directory listed 15. Before the arrival of our current-day supermarkets, these groceries sold everything from gardening supplies and feed for farm animals to fresh eggs, produce, and fishing tackle.

My friend and fellow librarian Frieda Seu Quon shared with me her memories of being one of the first Chinese American students in her school system and of growing up in the Min Sang Company, her family's grocery. Notice the shelves of Mr. Seu's store, filled with all sorts of wonderful things. And more than enough bananas for Grandma Clark's baking!

Chinese grocery stores were a fixture in small towns and even larger cities all over the South. The Eng family has owned a store in Houston for many years. Their relatives opened groceries in Arkansas and San Antonio. These businesses were often passed from one generation to the next and remained in the same family for many years.

*Mr. George Seu and his family at their Min Sang Company grocery in Greenville, Mississippi, in the late 1940s. This store has likely been in continuous operation longer than any other in the region. Photo courtesy of Frieda Quon.*

*George Eng at the register of his grocery store, George's Lucky 7, in Houston, Texas, at about the same time (1948-1958) that Billy works in his great-uncle's store. Photo courtesy of the Eng family.*

How did so many Chinese immigrants come to settle in the South, and especially in the Mississippi Delta region? Shortly after the end of the Civil War, some came to work as farm laborers. They quickly took over the role of the old plantation commissary stores and began operating neighborhood groceries, serving both black and white clientele.

They learned English from their employers, from reading newspapers, and from running their own businesses. They established churches and were consistently excellent students. But in the years before civil rights legislation was passed, the South had segregated schools, restaurants, and many public places. After a 1927 Supreme Court case classified Chinese American students as "colored," some

*The Chinese Mission School, soon after its opening.*
*Photo courtesy of Delta State University's Mississippi Delta Chinese Heritage Museum.*

communities did not allow them to attend the segregated white schools. This led Chinese American parents to educate their children in churches and homes, and even to build boarding schools. Often, families moved to school districts where they were welcome, much as Billy Wong's parents sent him to live in my fictional town of Paris Junction, Arkansas.

Although I changed the closing date, I based the high school Billy's older sister and brother attended on the Cleveland, Mississippi, Chinese Mission School (1937–1951), a boarding school for Chinese American youngsters of all ages. The memories of many of its students were vibrantly brought to life in the book edited by Paul Wong and Doris Ling Lee, *Journey Stories from the Chinese Mission School* (2011).

By the time I was in school in the 1960s, Chinese American students were part of the public school system and were involved in sports, clubs, and activities. In fact, my friend Bobby Moon and I served together on the staff of our school's newspaper, the *Cleveland Hi-Lite*.

One of my favorite quotes about historical fiction comes from another writer. In his book *Catch You Later, Traitor*, Avi writes, "History is memory researched. Historical fiction is memory brought to life."

Yes, this is a story I made up. But it's based on the memories of a lot of us, as well as on my own research. Many smart writers and readers helped me understand the story behind *Making Friends with Billy Wong*. I hope my book will bring this little-known part of our country's history to life.

# Acknowledgments

Much as Azalea's journey started with an invitation, this story began with something I read. My high school friend Bobby Joe Moon published an essay based on his letter to a young family member about growing up in the Mississippi Delta during the 1950s and '60s. Although his story and Billy's are not the same, he was quick to answer questions over many, many months. I also consulted Frieda Seu Quon, who has been instrumental in building and growing the Mississippi Delta Chinese Heritage Museum on the campus of Delta State University.

Without Bobby and Frieda and their resources and memories, this story could have quickly become sidetracked onto the road to ruin, much like Azalea fears for her summer.

When this story was a mere idea waiting for inspiration, my friend Julie Eastwick shared gardening and good-manners tips, as well as her best china. Thank you, Julie, for brainstorming over cups of delicious French tea.

A special thanks to Beth Boswell Jacks, the first professional writer who offered my words a home.

My agent, Linda Pratt, pens encouraging thoughts on beautiful notepaper and also gives pep talks. Everyone needs a Linda in her life.

To my SCBWI Tampa Bay critique group, you rock, Skyway Writers. And I will always cherish the early, remarkable advice from my New Jersey writer friends. Please, keep up the cheering.

*Making Friends with Billy Wong* would still be languishing inside my computer were it not for the good people at Scholastic, especially my editor, Andrea Davis Pinkney, and the amazing publicity and events teams. They are brilliant, supportive, and a whole lot of fun. Thank you! You inspire me more than you can imagine.

# About the Author

Augusta Scattergood is the author of *Glory Be*, which was a National Public Radio Backseat Book Club selection, a Texas Bluebonnet Award nominee, and hailed by Newbery medalist Richard Peck as the story of a bygone era "beautifully recalled." Her novel *The Way to Stay in Destiny* was named an Amazon Best Book of the Month. A children's book reviewer and former librarian, Ms. Scattergood has devoted her life and career to getting books into the hands of young readers. Her reviews and articles have appeared in the *Christian Science Monitor*, *Delta Magazine*, and other publications. Ms. Scattergood, who lives in St. Petersburg, Florida, is an avid blogger. To learn more, visit www.augustascattergood.com.